THE PUNISHMENT OF IVY LEAVOLD

SIERRA SIMONE

THE PUNISHMENT OF IVY
LEAVOLD

CHAPTER 1

JULIAN

*S*he was gone.

    She was really gone.

Ivy Leavold had left me—left me and Markham Hall and had gone to find the family I'd hidden from her—which was something I didn't regret.

I only regretted not doing a better job.

I had tried to give her space as she'd packed and as Gareth had readied the carriage to take her to York. She wouldn't hear of taking any money, she said that solicitor—damn him to hell—would help her, but I still folded two or three hundred pounds into her purse when she wasn't looking. Then I walked to the library and locked the door, taking the entire decanter of scotch into the window seat with me so I could drink as I watched her leave.

It felt like it took only seconds, even though I knew it had been nearly an hour between her whispering *I'm leaving* and the carriage wheels rolling out of the courtyard. An hour between me sliding inside of her and her walking out of my life.

No, *our* life.

God was punishing me, I was sure of it. It wasn't enough that I would burn after death. He wanted to punish me now—strip away the only thing that mattered to me. Three months ago, nothing mattered. Not my estate or my wealth. Even my friends weren't enough to color the gray-washed days of my existence.

But then Ivy came, and I felt something again. Something that wasn't anger or shame or the emptiness I'd begun to cultivate as carefully as a gardener cultivates his garden. I felt curiosity at first, along with the urge to shield her and take care of her. And then desire. And then love.

And now loss.

I drank until all the thoughts left my mind, stumbled to the sofa and knew no more.

* * *

IVY

I'd been to London twice as a girl with my parents, but nothing prepared me for the choking, bustling mess that greeted me when I alighted from the train platform. People swarmed around me, pushing and yelling, and I had to blink against the smoky air that pervaded every corner of the station.

"Miss Leavold?"

It was an older man, perhaps in his fifties, in a smartly pressed suit and with the officious air of a servant. I knew at once he must be the person my aunt Esther had sent to collect me.

I nodded.

"Good. Shall we proceed? Your trunk has been arranged for."

With a last look at the train, the train that had borne me all the way from Yorkshire and had been the location of many quiet tears, I nodded. This was my life right now. In a strange town with strange people.

Without Mr. Markham.

* * *

ESTHER LEAVOLD LIVED in a small but fashionable house on Gilbert Street, barely a stone's throw away from Grosvenor Square. It was hard not to be nervous as our carriage stopped and as the servant led me inside the front foyer. I didn't know what to expect; I had never met this Esther Leavold and I couldn't remember ever hearing much of her, although since she had spent the last thirty or so years in India, I supposed it wasn't inconceivable that she wouldn't have been spoken of much by my parents. And Thomas barely spoke about anything at all, unless it was to chastise me for talking too much or for spending too much time outdoors.

Nevertheless, I walked into 27 Gilbert Street expecting an old woman and instead encountered someone who did not look so much older than myself.

She was petite and wildly curvy, with rounded breasts and hips and a small waist, and with her blonde hair twisted up into the fronted curls that were so fashionable here in London. She was perhaps in her mid-thirties, but this was only a hazarded guess, because her tiny bow mouth and bright blue eyes gave the impression of a child. And the energy with which she swept into the foyer and gathered me into an embrace—that seemed very childlike too.

"Hel-hello," I said, my breath choked from her tight hug. "Thank you for—"

She let me go and waved a hand. "No, no. No thank yous, please. It's bad enough to come to England and not know anyone, and even worse to discover that any relations you can presume upon for company are dead. You are doing me the favor by coming to stay with me. It's quite lonely, you know, being unmarried at my age."

I caught a glimpse of the silver dish on her table, filled to the brim with calling cards. *Not that lonely*, I thought as she led me into the front room and rang for tea.

"Now, I know you must be exhausted from the journey, but I really must insist you take something to fortify yourself before you rest, and also we must make plans for tonight and tomorrow. The Lady Samantha Haverford has invited me to dinner and I think I should bring you along. What a perfect place to introduce you to the important people here—and I know what you're thinking, Ivy, you're wondering how I can know since I've only come from Bombay eight weeks ago, but Lady Haverford was introduced to me by Colonel Barnes—a former beau, if you must know, but really a good man—and Barnes always has the best taste in refined company." She stopped to a take a breath —possibly the first she'd taken since I walked in the door.

A dinner party with London society sounded unbearable— especially given how close to tears I'd felt all day. It was impossible to entertain the idea. "I'm sorry, but I really am so tired," I said, not trying to hide the warble in my voice. Let her think it was exhaustion and not my broken heart.

She responded immediately, her face pulling into a concerned pout. "Of course! You poor dear. We will wait until tomorrow then—the Hermanns from Vienna are having a garden party. Do you have a proper afternoon dress? No? I thought not. The solicitor who helped me find you told me about how my nephew gambled away all your money. Shameful. Not to worry though. I have plenty of money for the both of us, and we shall go shopping this week. Now, to your room! You must tell me if you like it, or if you would like anything changed, or even if you want to switch rooms—there are plenty in this house."

The maid came into the room bearing tea, but Esther pushed past her, my need for fortification apparently forgotten. I didn't mind much—the swaying motion of the train and the violent emotions I couldn't suppress had left me feeling a little queasy.

We went upstairs, Esther chattering the whole way. I learned that she was the product of a late marriage between my grandfather and a diplomat's daughter, whom he had met while traveling for business. When he'd died several years back, he'd directed that the shares of his company went to his daughter, and so now Esther was quite the heiress. Perhaps a year ago, I would have felt resentful that my grandfather hadn't thought to bequeath any money to the children from his first marriage, Violet's father and my own. But now I hardly cared. After all, if things hadn't happened the way they had, then I wouldn't have gone to Markham Hall. I wouldn't have fallen in love with Mr. Markham.

And I couldn't regret any of that. Not yet.

Esther pointed me to a door, and we entered what was to be my room. How Esther could ever imagine I could complain about it, I had no idea. If anything, it was *too* luxurious, hung with richly colored portraits and dominated by a massive canopy bed. Everything was upholstered in silks and damasks, all deep plums and vivid greens.

"I had it done up as soon as I bought the house, knowing that you would have to come live with me, circumstances being what they are. I did not know your taste, but I did my best and— darling, *is that a ring?*"

I had placed my hand on the back of the low sofa in front of the fireplace, and the sunlight pouring in from the window caught my engagement ring, sending gleams of light around the room. I had not made any effort to hide it; in fact, I had been under the impression that my aunt knew about my engagement.

"Yes," I said, feeling a low flicker of amusement at Esther's gaping mouth, a sort of joyless mirth that vanished immediately. "I thought perhaps Solicitor Wickes would have told you . . . ?"

"Why, certainly not!" Color was rising in Esther's cheeks. "Can you imagine? He knew and he didn't tell me, when he knows I have not a soul in the world to lay claim on! But my dear, if you are engaged, when are you to be married? And when shall I meet this man? Tell me, is he quite handsome? And his figure—what is it like? I prefer the ones who are broad in the shoulder, the ones who can carry me, which let me tell you, is not every man." She raised her eyebrows, tapping a small foot under her dress. "Answer me, my dear. When are you to be married?"

There was a peculiar ball at the back of my throat, and if I spoke, it would turn all of my words into quavering tears. But I couldn't stop them anyway, and they started to fall hot and fast down my cheeks.

"Oh my," Esther clucked, coming toward me and folding me into another crushing hug. "What did he do, the cad? Did he reject you because of your poverty? Or lack of breeding? Or did he—" her eyes danced with pre-emptive righteous anger "—did he carry on with another woman? What a beastly scoundrel! Well, not to worry, my dear, you are here with me now, and I guarantee you that if I did not know of this engagement, then society does not know of it, and your reputation will come out unscathed. And you are so young and pretty and with me at your side—yes, we will find you a proper husband in no time."

In a way, I liked how Esther didn't need me to respond to her. I could allow her to do all the talking while I struggled against these unreasonable tears, these tears that refused to dissipate no matter how many of them I cried. But I had to tell her that it wasn't what she thought. I had to defend Mr. Markham.

"He didn't do anything like that," I said, hating how sniffly my voice sounded. "He—I just. It's complicated. I thought I could stay here for a while, you know, while I thought about things."

Esther forced my head onto her shoulder. "You take as long as you need, dearie, you understand? You can stay right here, and I will take care of you."

"Thank you," I said into her dress. It felt wrong to be taken care of in this way. *It won't last,* I promised myself. I'd make myself useful, or at the very least, self-sufficient.

Why hadn't it felt wrong for Mr. Markham to take care of me, emotionally and sexually and in all the other ways I'd needed? Was that further evidence of how corrupted I was?

"You must tell me his name, at least," my aunt insisted. And she took my shoulders and pushed me back from her so she could look me in the eye. "Ivy. Who is this man?"

There was no point in avoiding the question—she would either keep asking or find out through some other means. "Julian Markham," I said, my voice cracking. "Julian Markham of Markham Hall. In Yorkshire."

Her eyebrows knit together for a moment. "Markham . . . " she said, as if trying to recall where she'd heard the name before.

"Violet's husband," I supplied dully.

"But Violet died only a few months ago, did she not? How on earth did he manage to court you in such a short time? You should have both been in mourning!"

Her outrage over the breach of etiquette seemed so petty next to everything else. How outraged would she have been to learn that Julian had once punished Violet by making her watch as he fucked another woman? How worried would she be if she knew that Julian was long suspected of Violet's murder? Whatever she thought she could assess about the situation, she didn't know the half of it.

"I had to live with him—I had nowhere else to go," I said. "And then . . . it just happened."

It just happened. Nothing was further from the truth. It had been weeks of longing, of desire, punctuated with heady kisses and caresses. It had been desperate and perfect and all-consuming; it had been the only time I'd felt truly alive. Nothing about it was "just." Nothing about it simply happened by chance.

Esther regarded me, the kind of hungry look that I'd grown used to from Mrs. Harold, the rector's wife. A look hungry for information, for stories, for juicy details. But unlike Mrs. Harold, Esther also radiated an affection and a compassion that —while shallow—was still kindly meant. When she saw that I wasn't going to say any more, she patted my arm. "Don't worry. I will take care of everything. You take tonight and rest. If you want, I can stay home from Lady Haverford's . . . ?"

There was a bit of reluctance at the way she offered, and I saw her sigh of relief when I told her, "That is kind, but there is no need. I plan on sleeping most of the evening away—I wouldn't notice if you were here or not."

"Well, don't hesitate to ask for anything while I'm gone. And I'll be sure to check in on you when I come home!"

With a swift kiss on the cheek, Esther departed and I finally had the room to myself. And in the silence, all of the thoughts and worries and pains came flooding in. How Julian had kept my aunt from me. How viciously he had tormented Violet the night she died.

I closed my eyes against the image of him driving into the rector's wife, a look of cruel triumph on his face. I closed my mind against the spike of dark, dark lust the image inspired in me.

And that was the real reason I had fled so suddenly—what all this meant about *me*. Normal women didn't feel the way I did, I was certain. They weren't excited by acts of barely restrained brutality. They didn't purr at the thought of being called a pet, a kitten. They didn't feel that any amount of submission or possession was worth seeing that perfect, vulnerable soul inside the man, and I did. Everything that Julian did, to me and to others, energized and enlivened me. Sometimes with fear, sometimes with lust, sometimes with unrelenting waves of love. But why was I okay feeling fear mingled with all these emotions?

Because deep down, you always truly felt safe.

And especially now that he had confessed the truth of what happened the night my cousin died, of how his revenge on her infidelity had driven her to rush into that fatal horseback ride, I knew that he wasn't a murderer. That my body had always been safe from him. Safe *with* him.

But what about my heart? Could I trust that he wouldn't turn that barbarism on me? Would I be able to withstand the onslaught of his darkness?

Or was I just as dark?

And even if we could work our way through all of this, what if I no longer satisfied him? What if I couldn't perform the way he wanted me to, couldn't be a good pet?

Hollowness flooded through me, chasing out everything else. And what did it matter in the end? I had left, and while I had given him permission to follow me, I didn't know that he would. Julian Markham was a proud man.

My trunk had already been placed inside, so I stripped out of my traveling dress, unhooked my corset and petticoats, and changed into a fresh chemise. I washed my hands and face and then I crawled under the blankets of the bed. Even though it was only late afternoon, I knew once I closed my eyes, I would fall asleep. And I did.

CHAPTER 2

JULIAN

J gave her two days. Of course, I followed her to London as soon as I could, my valet insisting on coming with me in what I saw as a fit of loyal pique, and I obtained the address of this Esther Leavold as soon as humanly possible. But I didn't go there.

Not yet. I would allow Ivy as much space as I could possibly stand.

Which to be honest, wasn't much. I had barely slept since she'd left, my every thought consumed by her. I missed her wild laugh, her defiant smile. I missed the way her body had come to life under my touch, as if she were a treasure only I could unlock.

Just the thought sent a spike of heat through me. God, what I wouldn't give for her to be with me now. I would kiss my way up those perfect thighs, those thighs that were strong and lithe but still impossibly soft, and then I would bury my face in her cunt. I would lick and nip at her until her back was arched and her feet were pushing uselessly against the floor, and then I would seal my mouth over her clit and suck until she came. And while she was still riding the waves of her orgasm, I would shove into her, hard. She liked her fucking rough, with the edge of pain on the periphery, and I loved watching her come apart in my hands, her hips bucking and her eyes delirious. Her perfect lips parted. I would make her come on my cock one more time before I surrendered myself, before I pumped her full of my seed.

I was hard just thinking about it, but I ignored the urge to stroke myself off, to blunt the edge of ever-present hunger I had when it came to Ivy. It would be a paltry substitute. It would be no substitute at all. And I had never been one to accept anything less than what I wanted.

And if I was honest with myself, I didn't want to ease any of my pain, physical or emotional. I wanted to hurt, I wanted to be miserable. I wanted to hate every moment that I wasn't with her.

I looked around the opulent hotel room that I had rented only a short walk away from Esther Leavold's house. I knew Molly and some of the others were in town, but I had no desire to see them. Molly had little patience for romantic love and so would be impossible. The others had no experience with this kind of attachment at all—their love lives stopped at dalliances and brief courtships. Even Silas didn't truly understand, although he had been the only one to truly stay by my side while I'd chased after Violet.

Pointlessly chased after Violet.

I ground the heels of my hands into my eyes. *Fuck.* Just thinking of it made me furious and devastated and ashamed all at once. I wanted to say that she had broken my heart with her infidelity, but that wasn't quite true, because by that point I'd realized that I didn't love her in the slightest. No, it had been my honor and my pride that had been wounded, and in a way that made my actions all the more reprehensible, because I couldn't even claim to have been blinded with heartbreak.

The horrified look in Ivy's eyes as I had told her . . .

But in a way, it had been such a huge relief. This sin I had carried with me, had borne alone. Silas knew that something had happened with Mrs. Harold, but gentle soul that he was, he had no idea that it hadn't been the ordinary extramarital tryst. Even he, my oldest friend, would be aghast.

I stood and started pacing the large room. How was it on the heels of my worst moments, my darkest sins, I had stumbled upon the one person I had been unconsciously searching for my entire life? The time in my life when I least deserved love and goodness, and then Ivy had appeared, wary and distant and perfect.

I had known from the moment I held her wrist and felt the blood thrumming there, the moment I saw the pulse fluttering in her neck. I had known that there was something different in her, something that I responded to on such a deep level that it was impossible to control my reactions to it. But how could I take her, as at my mercy as she was? If I despoiled my dead wife's cousin, only a month after her death, then I would be that same monster who had fucked another woman for revenge. No —I had vowed to myself to protect her, no matter how much I wanted her. I was a better man than that.

But I hadn't counted on her wanting me too. And truthfully, I was *not* a better man than that. How could I claim to be, when I still hated the memory of Violet, when I still didn't know if I would honestly go back and undo what I had done the night she died? When I couldn't even truly let Ivy go, when I had promised her I would?

She said it was okay to follow her, I reminded myself.

Which was good. Because I couldn't wait any longer.

* * *

14

IVY

I had been trying to draft a letter for about three hours, and so far it only read *Dear Julian* at the top. I didn't know what I wanted to say, really, and even more than that, I wasn't sure what I *should* say. Should I tell him that it was best if we dissolved our engagement? My aunt Esther seemed to think so, and she had spent the last day and a half reminding me. This would have been the wisest option, according to every bit of conventional wisdom I knew.

But I couldn't write the words. Every time I started, a wave of exhaustion and nausea would crash over me and I would lay down my pen and stare out of the window, letting melancholy thoughts chase themselves over and over again.

But how could I write anything else? If I wrote how I really felt—how lonely and lost and empty—if I told him how I spent my days in London, barely eating and listlessly watching the street outside the window, then he would take that as encouragement. Confirmation. And that was as unfair to him as it was to me.

A knock at the door. My new lady's maid, Polly, came in. "A caller in the receiving room, Miss Leavold."

"It's for my aunt, surely," I said, turning back to my unwritten letter.

"It's a gentleman. I told him you wouldn't be able to receive him since your aunt wasn't home, but he insisted. He said you were engaged to be married."

My head snapped up, adrenaline flooding through me. *Julian.*

"Should I tell him to leave or . . . ?"

"No," I said, standing and giving my reflection a cursory inspection. I looked pale and tired, but there was nothing to be done about it at the moment. "I'll be right down."

I smoothed my dress and went down the stairs, swallowing back my trepidation and excitement.

How desperately I wanted to see him. And how desperately I wanted him to go away.

I caught my breath as I entered the room. He stood by the window, the light framing his tall body, catching in his too long hair, every edge and line of him sharp and clear, as if he were somehow more real than everything else around him. It was as if I'd seen everything through a veil since I'd left Markham Hall, seen everything in the sepia tone of photographs, and he was the first truly vivid and detailed thing I'd seen in days. He turned at my entrance, his eyes drinking me in, his mouth parting slightly. His fingers twitched by his side, and I thought of all the times they'd traced circles around my breasts, slid deeply into my cunt.

Not even thirty seconds in the same room with him and I was wet.

He knew, somehow he knew, because he crossed over to me in a few quick strides and slanted his mouth over mine, pressing his warm lips against my hungry ones, parting them and licking into my mouth with a ferocity that made my knees weak.

"God, wildcat," he whispered. "I've missed you so much. I've missed the way you taste."

And then his lips moved down my neck, kissing the silk swell of my breast, the corseted nip of my waist, going down to his knees and sliding his hands up my legs.

I knew what he was going to do as soon as he lifted the hem of my dress and tugged the interfering underclothes away. I should have said no. I should have said that we had to keep away from each other until we could make decisions about our future. But the tired apathy was blasted away in his intense presence, leaving only a quickening pulse and a growing hunger in its wake. So what I said instead was, "Someone will see . . . "

"Let them," he said, looking up into my eyes. I'd imagined those eyes so many times the last few days, thinking perhaps I was exaggerating how green they were, how expressive they were. But if anything, I hadn't done them justice. They were a vibrant emerald that painters would murder for and framed by long dark lashes that fluttered now as his fingers found the sensitive skin between my thighs.

I couldn't stop the moan that left my mouth.

"Your pussy is so wet for me," he said, his fingers running softly over my skin, stopping here and there to delve deeper or rub a little harder. "Why won't you come home to me so I can take care of it all the time?"

I was already so upset, so worked up, and here he was, his stubbled jaw and his haunted eyes making him look more desperately delicious than ever, and my body had been keening for him for what felt like years . . .

"Oh, you're going to come, Ivy. Let me taste it. Let me taste you." Without waiting for my response, he raised my skirts and pressed his lips to my swollen clitoris. Just the soft kiss made me buckle and gasp, but then his tongue licked out, tasting my flesh, and I truly cried out. I laced my fingers in his hair, not caring how tightly I pulled, just needing him to stay exactly where he was, exactly where I wanted him, and then my climax erupted and I came violently on his mouth. His arms wrapped tight around me, supporting me as I rode out the waves as silently as I could, still distantly aware that we were in an open room in a house full of servants.

After I finished, he rearranged my skirts and stood. I put my finger on his lips and then brought it to my own mouth and licked it.

He groaned.

I wanted more. I wanted more of him, more of us and our pleasure and our sweat. And right now, I didn't care about anything else. All the doubts, all the questions, they could wait for just another handful of minutes. It was like I was a sleeping queen in a fairy tale, brought to life by the right man's kiss, and I felt so very, very awake right now, so very alive. What was that shadow world of doubt and worry compared to this? What queen would choose a twilight slumber alone when they could consort with the king who brought them to life?

But of course, I wasn't a queen.

I was a wildcat.

I put my hand on his chest and roughly pushed him back until his knees hit the sofa and he sat. He helped me free his dick from his pants, and then I was climbing on top of him, impaling myself on the iron heat of his shaft. I sank all the way down until he was completely buried in me.

He made to speak again, but I stopped him with a hungry kiss. "No words," I said. "Please." And then I ground myself against him, feeling his cock sink even deeper, and began rubbing my clit against him as hard as I could. I rode him with everything I had, rode him with all the pent-up emotions I'd found it so difficult to grapple with. I expended them all on him, I unleashed every ounce of longing and betrayal and anger. I scratched his arms, pulled at his hair, bit his neck. And he took it, his eyes hooded as he watched me work myself on him, wrench my pleasure from him. And I did get my pleasure, biting him on the neck one last time before I started shuddering and clenching on top of him, feeling more free and clear of heart than I had since before I left.

Only he gave this to me, I realized. This three-dimensional world, this open world, and only with him could I be myself completely. In the haze of pleasure, it was so easy to ask myself *why did I run?*

Why?

Mr. Markham held me carefully as I came down, but when I finally opened my eyes, I could read the look on his face as clearly as if he had spoken aloud.

My turn.

His hands found my waist, those long fingers almost meeting in the middle, and he lifted me up and slammed me back down, the force of it making me grunt. He didn't go easy on me—

It was as if he were punishing me in the same way I had just punished him. I surrendered myself to his impressive strength and let myself be carried away by it. By him and his brute force.

By the huge cock that jabbed into me over and over again. By the waves of uncontrollable emotion that rolled through me.

And I couldn't help the heat pricking at my eyelids when I felt him stiffen and then start pulsing inside of me. Oh God, it felt so damn perfect. But that was the problem, wasn't it? When we were fucking, our world was perfect. When our bodies were joined, everything but our love melted away, refined into gold by the furnace of our desire.

But we couldn't always be fucking. We had to live lives. We had to coexist for decades, we had to see other people, and one day we would have to have children.

I loved him. I wanted him by my side, always. More than anything. But the things he had done, and the truths he had hidden—how could I willingly embrace all of that and carry it into a marriage?

I didn't know that I could.

His hands tightened on my waist as I lifted my hand. The light, as always, caught the ring and threw glinting arcs of color around the room. There had been a time when I'd imagined it on my finger until the end of my days, a cool weight on my hand as I fell into my final slumber, hopefully surrounded by children and grandchildren with the Markham green eyes. What a foolish fantasy. Girls like me—poor, without connections or property— didn't get their fairy-tale endings. I wasn't a queen. I wouldn't even be fit to serve a queen. I had always been destined for the gray world of isolation and solitude, and it had been stupid of me to ever think anything different.

I slowly tugged off the ring as he watched, and I put it in his inside jacket pocket. He was still inside me through it all, a deeply physical reminder of how empty I would feel without him.

"I will always love you," I said. "But I don't know how to live with you. When we are together, everything feels right. But what if I wake up one day and I'm like Violet? And you despise me?"

"That will never happen," he said fiercely.

19

"And Julian—" He froze at his name, as he often did. "I . . . you make me want strange things. The woman that I am becoming—I am frightened by her. I don't think I can live my life with the kind of desires I have with you."

He didn't let go of my waist. "You are becoming more like yourself, Ivy. And only I can give you what you need."

I slid off of him, wrestling out of his grasp. I took in everything about him, drank him in for what would probably be the last time: his lanky frame, square jaw, thick eyebrows. I touched his face, laying my hand against his high cheekbone and feeling the stubble tickle my palm. He closed his eyes, pressing into my touch.

"Goodbye, Mr. Markham."

CHAPTER 3

JULIAN

THREE WEEKS LATER...

"So the rumors *are* true."

I blinked against the sudden wash of sunlight in the hotel room. I'd been slumped in a chair in front of the fireplace, debating the merits of having a drink this early in the morning. I wasn't normally the type to seek solace in drunkenness, but I would be lying to myself if I didn't admit how appealing the feeling was. The feeling of forgetting.

Silas hurled himself into the chair across from me, all charm and smiles like always. "At least you don't smell. I was worried that I would have to come dunk you forcibly into a bath and burn your clothes." He looked around the room. "I'm actually impressed, Markham. You are quite a tidy little hermit."

"What are you doing here?" I asked tiredly. "How did you even get in?"

"I told the concierge I was your brother and I was worried

21

for your health. And then I handed him some money. You know, the usual."

"But why . . . " I trailed off, already exhausted by the exchange. What did it matter? What did anything matter? Ivy had ended our engagement, not seconds after we'd stopped shivering through our climax, and I couldn't bring myself to care about anything else. Even the thought of leaving London for my own house seemed untenable—no matter how sundered we were practically, I couldn't tear myself away geographically. I spent my days imagining hers. Was she walking in Hyde Park now? Visiting the British Museum? Spending time with her aunt?

"Molly said she saw your valet running errands and so she asked around, and word was that you were holed up in here brooding. And I said, 'Our Markham *brooding?* How out of character for him.'"

"Your sarcasm is duly noted."

Silas folded one long leg over the other, studying me for a moment. "What happened?" he finally asked. "You can tell me."

I wouldn't. It was unthinkable, laying bare the pain and shame once more by speaking it all out loud. But when I opened my mouth to tell him it was none of his business, the story started tumbling out. All jumbled together—Ivy breaking off the engagement, using Mrs. Harold as a weapon against Violet, the ever-present fear that I was indeed an evil man, and therefore Ivy deserved better. She deserved for me not to hunt her down. She deserved for me not to possess her. She deserved a life free from me.

But the trouble was, I couldn't live any kind of life without her.

Silas listened to the whole saga, punctuated with the frequent outbursts of my despair, and even though disgust flickered briefly in his eyes when I described what I had done to Violet the night she died, it wasn't followed with judgment. In fact, his voice was kind when he said, "Markham, my man, you've got to forgive yourself. Yes, you did something terrible, but we all saw how desperately unhappy you were. No one who spent any time with you and Violet could truly fault you for lashing out like that."

My face was in my hands at this point. "Ivy faults me."

He cleared his throat. "Have you seen her? You know, since she broke your heart and all?"

"No," I said into my fingers. "She made it very clear she doesn't want to see me." Then I thought a moment. "Wait, have *you* seen her?"

He shrugged. "That aunt of hers is parading her through every fashionable house in London. She's out every night."

My chest squeezed. She was out—laughing? Drinking? Dancing? With other people?

With other men?

"She seems to hate every minute of it," Silas said softly. "In case you were torturing yourself."

He knew me so well.

"I saw her at the Rochefords two nights ago. She's lost weight, she's got dark circles under her eyes, she barely talks. I asked around, and while it seems her aunt is hell-bent on making Ivy this season's prize, Ivy is not at all interested. She has not danced once since she's arrived and has refused most callers."

How funny. I had hated the idea that she was gallivanting about town, being courted by other men. But I also hated that she was unhappy. I wanted to wrap her in blankets and make her sleep away those dark circles. I wanted to feed her from my fingertips until her flesh became supple and soft again.

"Of course, given this new fortune she's tied to through her aunt, and—let's be honest here, Markham—even with the weight loss and the tired look, she is still quite beautiful, she's become the most talked about girl in town. Who is this new gorgeous girl who is suddenly so rich? And what is the mysterious tragedy that haunts her?"

"Why shouldn't they talk about her?" I murmured. "She *is* beautiful. Captivating."

"Snap out of it," Silas ordered. "You aren't a complete martyr yet. And I have some hopeful news for you."

"What is that?"

"I talked to her. I talked to her for quite a long time. And she is still hopelessly in love with you."

I looked up, my stomach jumping. "She is?"

"Of course she is, you idiot. But I think she's frightened of you."

"God." My head sank into my hands again. "She should be. What kind of man am I, to do the things I do and expect her to stay devoted to me?"

"Stop wallowing. I'm not finished." He waited until I looked up at him. "You are pretty terrible, but I think the real problem is that she is frightened of herself. She's frightened of who she is with you. You may be twisted, but you reveal to her that deep down, she is too."

"She said all that?"

Silas grinned. "Well, not in so many words."

"It doesn't matter. She said the same thing to me when she ended our engagement." I stood up, suddenly too agitated to sit still. "Nothing has changed. She still can't bear to be with me."

"No," Silas said. "She thinks that she's not *supposed* to bear being with you. She's like you, Markham, she's scared that somehow she's tainted inside. Evil. But you and I know that's not the truth. It's up to you to show her that she already *is* the kind of woman who can love you, that she already has those tastes and passions peculiar to you, and that nothing about that is evil."

I stopped by the window, looking out over the street. Silas was right, but I didn't know that it made a difference. Ivy had made a decision, and even though it would kill me, I loved her enough to abide by it.

"Listen to me," Silas said, standing to join me. "This is not her saying that she doesn't love you. This is her saying that she's scared to."

"I know all this. But I can't force her to see that."

"Who said anything about forcing?" He turned and leaned back against the windowsill so that he was facing me. "Look, I'm just saying that you can *show* her that you are still here, that you are ready and waiting for her if she changes her mind. Show her that your devotion is unabated and that it can actually survive even if you aren't fucking constantly."

I frowned. "I don't like the idea of hovering around, being a menace. She wanted space away from me. Trying to insert myself into her social life to prove that I love her seems like the opposite of what she wants."

Silas held up his hands. "I'm not talking about stalking her every move. You have standing invitations to most of the places she's going to, correct? Go there in your own capacity, socialize with your own acquaintances. If she's there, then ask her if you can dance with her, dine with her, speak with her. Let her know that it's not a promise, it's not a contract. It is just your time and company, with no strings attached. If she says no, then you have your answer. But she may say yes."

"But she may not." But then I remembered something just then, something she'd said when she left Markham Hall.

I'm not using our signal . . .

We were still within the boundaries we had set with each other this summer. I was still her teacher, she was still my pupil.

She was still mine.

I lifted my head. Christ, why hadn't this occurred to me before? I had made it clear that until she had spoken it, our word, then I was free to do with her as I pleased.

This realization must have shown on my face, because Silas smiled and clapped me on the shoulder. "That's the spirit! After all, what do you have to lose?"

* * *

IVY

If I had ever regretted not having a proper debut in town, I didn't now. The last three weeks had been a flurry of afternoon teas, dinner parties that lasted well past midnight, and balls that lasted even longer than that. Not to mention the dress fittings, visits to the haberdasher and milliner, and the endless hours I spent being prodded and primped by Esther's staff of capable maids.

I'd tried to beg off. I was tired, I wasn't feeling well, and I could barely hold a conversation longer than five minutes. But Esther was a formidable opponent, either ignoring my complaints or arguing with them until I was worn down—which admittedly wasn't difficult. I'd felt so bled dry after ending the engagement...as if severing myself from Mr. Markham had in turn severed something essential in me. I was a machine that no longer worked properly, a watch without cogs, a compass without a magnet. Esther moved me from place to place and changed me from dress to dress like I was a doll, and I let her, because inside I felt just as vacant and inanimate.

When I had seen Silas two nights since, I had almost wept with relief. Talking to someone who knew Mr. Markham, who would see him again, who reminded me so much of him—it was cathartic. And awful. And wonderful.

So now, at whatever terrible ball Esther had brought me to tonight, I felt a similar feeling of relief and excitement when I saw Silas across the room, bracketed by the blonde pillars of beauty that were Rhoda and Zona.

" . . . Which is precisely why Oxford is making a mistake letting the women in to study." I realized the speaker of this sentence was talking to me, one of the foppish young men that seemed all too eager to seize onto Esther's introductions. They seemed so *soft*—all striped pants and coiffed mustaches. The kind of men who, when married, would roll on top of their wives once a month and blindly poke for less than a minute before squirting and then falling asleep. My lip curled a little. These men were so unlike my Julian had been. I would never marry one.

Mustache mistook my expression as sympathetic disgust for his chosen conversational topic. "Exactly! You seem a reasonable woman, Miss Leavold. The fairer sex does not have the strength for that kind of rigorous study." His chest swelled. "That is, of course, why they should be shepherded into the care of a husband directly after leaving home. To leave home for school and then spend several unmarried years studying . . . it seems like such a dangerous undertaking."

My eyes were following Silas from across the room. I had to go to him, I had to know if he had spoken to Mr. Markham since the other night. I was so hungry for any mention of him; even just his name would be a kind of psychic salve.

"Girls do it for boarding school, do they not?" I asked Mustache politely, my gaze still on Silas.

He smiled at me as if I were simple. "But a boarding school is not in such close proximity to a boys' school, Miss Leavold. The collegiate scholars will all be on the same campus—it seems a risky proposition."

"For what? For a girl's virginity?"

Oh, if Thomas could see me now. He'd always hated how direct and tactless I could be with my words, and I could tell by Mustache's slack jaw that I'd really outdone myself. Nobody ever even alluded to such things in polite company. But I didn't care. I didn't care about Mustache's good impression or the good impression of anyone in this room. I just wanted to find Silas and fill my empty heart with crusts of memories and stale news.

"Miss Leavold—" Mustache stammered.

"Excuse me," I said, leaving him to be shocked alone.

But when I pushed my way past a cluster of guests, expecting to see Silas on the other side, I found that someone else had come to the ball. Someone else stood, leaning against the wall, talking to Silas and the women and another clump of people I didn't know.

His black evening jacket stretched across his broad shoulders, narrowing into tails that highlighted the slender torque of his waist. The matching trousers clung temptingly to his legs and ass, and his long fingers twitched at his sides—the only sign of restlessness that I could detect. His posture was easy, and I could hear his laugh booming across the floor—a sound that made my heart flip not once, but twice.

He hadn't seen me, not yet, and while I should have been able to think rationally through this, I could not. All I could think about was getting away, fleeing for cover.

I backed up, eyes only on Mr. Markham, bumped into a matron and her half-blind husband, and then turned and fairly ran for the door. There was a terrace here, I knew, a small paved area that led out into a pleasant cluster of trees and flowers, and I needed to be outside. I needed to breathe.

Outside, the September air was cool and moist, a light fog rolling in from the river to fill in alleys and niches and the hidden spaces in between trees. There was hardly anyone out here, just a handful of women fanning themselves after an exerting dance and a couple trying to steal a moment away from their chaperones.

Mr. Markham was here. *Here*. With me.

But not for me. I chewed on my lip. He hadn't come and found me, he hadn't written ahead of time to tell me he was going to be present. In fact, it seemed almost as if he had just come to be with his friends. Had he?

Why was I so disappointed at that thought? *I* had been the one to walk away, to claim that we needed separate lives. So could I really be upset that he was indeed living a separate life?

Yes, I thought fiercely. Yes, because I had spent the last three weeks in torment, in agony, and it looked like he had barely thought of me at all.

Yes, because even though I kept telling myself I had done the right thing, the *safe* thing, I wasn't sure that I had. In fact, I had the unnerving suspicion that I *hadn't* done the right thing, for myself or for him.

But what could I do? How could I make myself feel okay with what he was—with what I was? No. As always, it was easier to run. Easier to hide. And now I wanted to run from here all together. I would find Esther and demand to go home, and then I would force myself to sleep and to forget that I had seen his face once again.

I turned to go back into the silk and noise of the ballroom, but there was someone in my way. Someone tall and lean and with green eyes that glowed like northern lights in the dark.

My breath left me at the same time a jolt of want shot through me, making my cunt pulse. My body knew what it wanted, my body had no reservations. It wanted to be taken roughly in hand, kneaded and licked and fucked. And just the thought of it drove out all other thoughts.

"Miss Leavold," he said, inclining his head. His voice was formal and distant. I cringed inwardly at the sound of it, hating that we had this new distance between us.

"Mr. Markham," I whispered.

"I wanted to know if I could claim a slot on your dance card tonight, if it's not already filled."

The question was so politely uttered, so within the bounds of normal etiquette, that it took my mind a minute to catch up. Mr. Markham and I had never conducted our interactions within the bounds of etiquette. *Ever.* And he wanted to dance with me? I hated how pitifully happy the thought made me.

"I don't dance," I said.

"I've heard."

He stepped forward into a pool of lantern light, and I could see that the boutonniere pinned to his jacket was none other than a sprig of bluebells. I sucked in a breath. "Bluebell" was our signal, the word I would use when I needed space from him. And at that moment, I realized I hadn't used it when I'd ended our engagement. I hadn't even thought to.

As if reading my mind, he said, "You never spoke our signal, Ivy. Why is that?"

"I don't know," I said breathlessly.

"Would you like to say it now?"

My body hummed at the closeness to his while my mind reeled with the same thoughts that had been reeling there for weeks. I should say it. I should deploy the one thing I knew he would respect. He wouldn't follow me then, and I'd never again be at risk of marrying Mr. Markham.

But I was so tired of missing him. I was so tired of running away from it all.

"No," I said softly. "I don't want to say it."

Even in the dark, I could see Mr. Markham's wide smile. I expected him to grab me, to kiss me, maybe even to fuck me right here in this garden, but instead he only asked, "So may I have that dance after all?"

CHAPTER 4

JULIAN

*H*olding Ivy in my arms was the most delicious kind of torture. I was determined to show her my restraint, my decorum, my tenderness, but it was nearly impossible when I could feel the slope of her back through her corset, when her slender fingers were circled tightly around mine. All I wanted was to press against her and to feel every curve of hers pressing back. I wanted to nibble and suck every inch of exposed flesh from her temple to her collarbone, and I wanted to kiss the delicate spot where her pulse flickered on her neck, kiss it until she could feel my kisses coursing in her veins along with her blood. I wanted to kneel at her feet and kiss my way up to her perfect pussy.

I wanted to worship her in every way she deserved to be worshipped.

That wasn't all, though. We were not one of those quotidian couples that could be satisfied by kisses and caresses; even if I could restrain myself from my darkest impulses, without them, Ivy would wilt and fade. She would drift away from me and from us, and if I won her back, I would not allow that to happen. If I won her back . . . the thought fed on itself, unfolding into entire scenes in my mind. She would have to be punished, I decided. Punished for breaking my heart and even more so for breaking her own heart, a heart that was still trusted to my keeping and instruction. It wasn't hers to do with as she wanted, it was mine, and I would show her that with every hot inch of myself stroking the inside of her ass. Or perhaps with my palm hitting her flank over and over again. Or perhaps I would bind her hands and feet with rope, make her watch as I lazily pumped myself to an orgasm she wouldn't be able to touch or taste.

Yes. I wanted to worship her the way she deserved, but she also deserved punishment, my recalcitrant wildcat, and if I brought her back to me, I would score her with every bite mark and handprint she deserved.

But she deserves this too, I reminded myself. She deserved to be courted. She deserved to be flattered and pampered and wooed and I had done none of those things at Markham Hall. I'd been so obsessed with protecting her from myself, and then when that became an impossibility, I'd lost any sense of control or boundaries. I lost everything to find her, and for a while it was perfect.

Perfect things never lasted.

We met and came apart and then met again, spinning wide circles on the floor. Ivy was unfamiliar with most of the dances since her worthless brother had never bothered to make sure that she had a proper upbringing, but I found I was resenting him less and less for that. For one thing, I didn't give a fuck if Ivy could dance or embroider or play an instrument. For another, her brother's neglect had allowed her to grow up unspoiled by the shallow pretensions of society. She had just grown up as *her*. She was all the more Ivy because it had only been her and her moldering library and her sea cliffs and her trees, and the thought of her any other way brought me acute pain.

She looked up at me then. "I'm sorry I have to fumble my

way through the steps," she apologized. "Thank you for being so patient with me."

She was thanking me for letting me hold her again? Fuck. I didn't deserve that.

I didn't deserve her. Even outside of the awful things I'd done, I still couldn't reach her rare vibrancy of being. Ivy Leavold belonged in a primeval forest somewhere, shrouded in fog, face painted with woad, with ritual fires and otherworldly spirits shimmering around her. Even here in this ballroom, she was so obviously other and apart from these two-dimensional Londoners that they could not keep their eyes off her. Did she notice, I wondered, how they watched her every move? How every smile and step was followed by a hundred stares?

They were trying to figure it out. What was it that set her so above the other ladies present? She was quite pretty, of course, but there were other pretty women here. Though she didn't speak often, when she did speak, whatever she said was arresting and intelligent, if sometimes unsettlingly direct . . . but again, she wasn't the only intelligent woman in the room.

No, it was something too ephemeral to name, an unfamiliar quality that these carp hardly ever saw in their fetid pool of dances and luncheons. It had taken me weeks to realize it, and I'd had the advantage of months alone with her.

Ivy wasn't *tame*. She was here dressed in the same clothes, wearing the same manners as everybody else, but they no more hid her nature than the bars of a cage hid that of a tiger's in the zoo. And the same way people were drawn to those tigers stalking agitated circles in their pens, they were drawn to Ivy. They wanted to be her, they wanted to domesticate her. Everybody was fascinated by her.

Mine.

My grip tightened on her momentarily and then I forced myself to relax. No, I was not going to win her back that way. I couldn't stay away from her, but I could also give her space and time. This had to be her decision. She had to *want* to come back to me. And I would honor whatever decision she ultimately made. Because while it frustrated me that she wasn't soft and pliable like every other girl I'd been with, that was what I loved about her. Her strength. Her wildness.

And I was foolish enough to believe that maybe I could have them both—her love and her unbroken nature.

"May I visit you at your aunt's house?" I murmured in her ear.

She flushed, whether from the proximity of my mouth or from the memory of what we had done before in her aunt's house, I didn't know. "Yes," she said. "You may visit."

God, she looked so delicious right now. Even with the circles under her eyes, even with the frame I could tell had grown thinner since she'd left our home.

I wanted to make her better. I wanted to heal her.

I also wanted to fuck her ass until she begged for forgiveness.

But. Restraint.

"I'd also like to extend an invitation. The Baron is having a party this week, and I think it would be lovely if you joined me."

She met my eyes and raised an eyebrow. "Is this the infamous Baron that Molly and Silas went to visit this summer?"

"Yes."

She hesitated. "What will the party be like?"

I wanted to lie. I wanted to tell her that it would be safe and sedate. But I had decided to invite her because it was precisely the opposite of those things. Because while it was important for me to show her that I would respect her need for physical and emotional space, it was just as important that I show her who she really was. She was like me. And like me, she wouldn't be happy until she accepted that part of herself.

"It will be wild," I told her. "It will be debauched. And it will make anything you've seen at Markham Hall seem very proper in comparison."

There. I saw it before it vanished—the faint wave of arousal at the very thought. Her pupils had dilated and her lips had parted. "I . . . do I have to participate if I go?"

"Not at all. You may merely enjoy the spectacle if you'd like."

"Will your friends be there?"

"Yes."

She bit her lip. "I'll think about it."

I withdrew a scarlet envelope from my jacket and pressed it into her hand. "There's no obligation to go. But if you choose to, simply present this at the door and you'll be allowed in. The address and time and dress code are specified inside."

Irritation colored her voice. She didn't like rules or constraints. Unless of course, I was the one constraining her. My cock stiffened at the memory of knotting her wrists with my tie. One day, I'd like to blindfold her again. Yes, one day soon. The anticipation made me grow even harder. I needed to go soon before I ended up fucking her right here on the dance floor.

"Yes, wildcat, a dress code. It's a masked party. And I might suggest that you avoid bringing your aunt." And with that, I dropped a kiss on her forehead, lingering just a second longer than was appropriate to breathe in the flowers and soap smell of her hair.

Her mouth opened, as if she were sucking in a breath at my touch, and I could see her pink tongue behind those fuckable lips. And because I couldn't help myself, I wrapped a hand around the back of her neck and whispered, "If you were still mine, my dick would be buried in that perfect mouth right now. If you were still mine, I'd bend you over the nearest chair and make all these guests watch as I ate your cunt and made you come in front of them like a little slut."

She did gasp then, unconsciously moving to press her body to mine, her body no doubt remembering how I always made good on all of my promises.

But I wouldn't let her grind against me to seek relief. If she wanted it, she'd have to come and get it.

I bowed to her and then walked away.

* * *

IVY

He left me in the middle of the dance floor, in the middle of a dance, and for a minute, all I could do was stare after him, conscious only of the way his lips had felt against my skin, of his dirty, filthy words.

Like a little slut.

I shivered. I was, wasn't I? Because, despite everything, I wanted to be his little slut still. If he had ordered me to my knees to suck him off right there on the ballroom floor, I would have done it.

But even though any fool could have sensed the naked desire sparking between us, he had never once actually slipped the bounds of propriety. His hands had never strayed and even his kiss had been chaste.

What was he doing?

And did I want him to stop?

Eventually, I became aware that I was blocking the path of other dancers, so I moved off the dance floor and back to the patio. I put my hands on the railing, and I remembered I still had the envelope in my hand. The Baron's party. A party I shouldn't bring my aunt to.

Curious, I started to open it.

"I wouldn't go flashing that around if I were you," Silas said, appearing from nowhere. He had a cigarette in one hand and a full champagne glass in the other. "This is for you," he said. "You were looking a little flushed dancing with Markham out there. I thought maybe you were thirsty."

I accepted the drink, although I didn't tell him that the flush was from arousal and not exertion. He probably already knew anyway.

He leaned against the railing, still smoking. "Anyway, if people see you with that envelope, mark my words: there will be gossip. Not that everyone isn't gossiping about you right now anyway, but it's all good gossip so far. With that envelope, you will create a reputation that will be hard to undo."

"Is the Baron that reviled?"

Silas nearly choked on his cigarette smoke. "Reviled? Hardly. The Baron's parties are the most exclusive parties in London. Everyone is dying to get in, and so of course those that don't get invited are bitter beyond belief. But it's the bitterness of the jealous. Those same people pander to the Baron and his friends constantly in order to be included in one of his fetes."

"Even though they know the parties he throws are not quite . . . proper?"

"It's *because* of that. It's London, Ivy, in the most exciting century to be alive. Why wouldn't people want to have a little fun? And the Baron guards his parties and his guests' privacy very carefully, so you can be assured that you can sit before the rector on Sunday without sweating."

I tucked the envelope into my dress, still undecided about whether I would go or not. I wasn't worried about my reputation so much as myself. If I went, would I find myself drawn to all the things I'd been trying to avoid? I knew I would.

Such temptation.

I turned to Silas. "What is Mr. Markham doing?"

"I beg your pardon?"

"Why is he being so . . . " I searched for the right word. "Well-behaved?"

"Are you complaining?"

My cunt still hummed with the need to be fucked, but my mind was mostly clear. Mr. Markham wanted me, but he was willing to do it on my terms. He was willing to keep himself apart from me. I could barely stand it, so I knew it had to be next to impossible for him. "I'm not complaining."

"He loves you."

"And I love him. But that doesn't make us right for each other."

"What does that even mean?"

I stared into the garden. "We don't bring out the best in each other. And he has a lot of 'not the best' inside of him."

"I suggest you examine your definition of 'best,' Ivy. Are you holding your relationship to a true moral rubric or to the moral rubric you think you should have?"

I frowned.

"How fully do you want to live your life? With all parts of yourself awake and feeling? Or with only the parts that some people think are decent? Jules woke you up—all of you—and now you're trying to go back to sleep. Do you really think that's the wisest?" Silas took a final pull off his cigarette and then flicked it onto the patio. "I hope to see you at the Baron's."

"I'll think about it," I said faintly, turning his words over in my mind.

Was I really trying to go back to sleep?

* * *

THE ENVELOPE BURNED a hole through my dress as Esther and I rode home. I was wrestling with this massive, planet-like question as we rolled through the London streets. Had Julian really woken me up? Was this a part of me that had always been around, simply waiting dormant for the right stimulus?

And if so, was it even possible to disown that part of myself?

"I heard the best gossip about your ex-fiancé today," Esther confided.

My ears perked up, but my mind was still fumbling with these questions that Silas had raised, all while I felt impossibly conscious of the envelope poking my corset through my dress. The choice to embrace the wild, sensuous Ivy. It was literally pricking at me.

"Well, it's not so much about him as about his first wife, Arabella Whitefield. Do you know of her?"

I thought of her sad-eyed miniature in the library. "Yes, I know of her."

"One of the wealthiest families in Yorkshire. Anyway, apparently, her father Josiah Whitefield was quite the philanderer. Bastards sprinkled all over the county. And before he died, he was raising one of them *in his house*. Can you imagine? Poor Arabella. Growing up next to a bastard."

Arabella had had much bigger problems, like being fatally ill, but I didn't mention that to Esther. I just made a neutral noise, which she took as encouragement to keep talking. I mostly ignored her, now that I knew the gossip wasn't about Mr. Markham, and debated about going to the party. Because it was a difficult debate. I wanted to go more than anything. And I didn't want to be a spectator. I wanted Mr. Markham to fuck me there. I wanted mouths and hands on me. I wanted people to watch me and I wanted to watch other people while Mr. Markham's face was between my legs.

But I shouldn't want those things.

And there was the crux of the problem. Silas claimed that I was trying to force myself back to sleep, but I wasn't sure. It was more like standing at the edge of a cliff and deciding whether or not to jump. Because with Mr. Markham, I couldn't be sure if I would survive or be dashed against the rocks.

" . . . and after they died, the estate got sold off, and the bastard got shunted somewhere else without a cent. Isn't that shocking?"

Esther had been talking this entire time. Reluctantly, I turned my attention to her. "It is sad to be sure. But shouldn't Mr. Whitefield have provided for him in the will, if he truly wanted to protect him?"

Esther nodded vigorously. "But they say after Arabella died, he lost his senses with grief. He doted on her, you see. And so he died not soon after. Pneumonia, the doctors said, but really everyone knows it was of a broken heart."

It was dark, so Esther couldn't see me roll my eyes. "I don't see what's so shocking about the story. I just assume almost every man of stature has a bastard child somewhere."

"You're right," Esther said. "But it's our job to balance the unfairness of all this philandering with knowledge. Men may be free to do what they like without getting in trouble with the church or the courts, but a woman's chief weapon is her tongue, and we can make sure no man escapes unscored by it."

Sometimes I really liked Aunt Esther. "It's a wonder you're still unmarried," I said, but I said it warmly, and she laughed.

"I simply haven't met a man that can handle me yet, my dear. But when I do, then I'll submit to the yoke immediately."

CHAPTER 5

JULIAN

*I*n my mind, I was biting Ivy's neck hard enough to make her cry out.

While I'd waited for Gareth to fetch my bluebells for the day, I'd constructed several perfect ways to punish my wildcat for running away. As I absentmindedly squeezed and stroked myself through the fabric of my pants, I dreamed all these ways up like houses and lived in them fully, resisting the urge to pull out my dick and truly bring myself relief. I didn't want it this way. I only wanted her.

I dreamed of things I would almost certainly do—tying her up, fucking her in the ass, wrapping one hand around that smooth column of a throat—and things I would never do. It was those things that had me desperate at the moment, the thoughts of things I had done with other women but that I would never be able to do with Ivy—not because they were anything but arousing to me or because I didn't think she would enjoy it, but because I was so fiercely possessive of her that sharing every part of her, cunt included, would drive me to a jealousy so vicious that I wouldn't be able to control myself.

But I lost myself in them now, picturing Ivy bent over a table and then tied that way, her legs spread and her sex exposed to anyone who wanted to see. I would let men I trusted —Silas, the Baron, Gideon—finally sample all of her. I'd watch them come inside her, I'd watch them take turns, I'd watch her face as the Baron thrust into her without a shred of mercy, and then I'd watch as she came apart with pleasure from the onslaught.

Fuck. Just the thought of using that many cocks to punish her was enough to make me nearly lose it in my pants, like a boy in school.

I took a deep breath and steered myself away from thoughts of my wildcat. Or at least thoughts of her naked. I was about to visit her, and when I did, I intended to honor my unspoken promise to court her properly, to win her back with the part of myself that wasn't all darkness, if such a part existed. I would prove my devotion to Ivy by being the kind of man she didn't think I could be. An honest one. A loving one.

But once I had her back, she'd better be prepared.

* * *

As I rode in the cab to her residence, I wondered if Ivy's aunt would like me. Approve of me. Part of me didn't care in the least, but the rational part of me knew that part of demonstrating the strength of my love for her would involve winning over her family as well. Her family of one.

As it turned out, she was the one waiting for me in the receiving room when I arrived at her house that afternoon, and I felt my stomach clench upon entering, because for a moment, I thought I was looking at Violet. The same blue eyes, the same fair hair. The same fine features straight from a painting. But then she smiled, and I relaxed. Esther was no doppelgänger.

Shorter and curvier, with a face much more disposed to happiness.

"Mr. Markham," she greeted, not making to stand. "Ivy will be down shortly. She went to lie down after her meal."

"Is she feeling well?"

Esther met my gaze with a frank expression. She may be a socialite, but she wasn't a simpleton. "I think we both know the answer to that. Now, I assume those are for me?"

I offered her the bouquet of white roses that—yes—I had brought as a bribe for her regard.

"Thank you." She examined them for a few seconds then dropped them on the couch next to her. "Now, have a seat, will you?"

I sat, leaning back and crossing my legs so that my ankle rested on my knee. I wasn't nervous, but I was anxious. I wanted to see Ivy. I wanted to touch her. Every moment since I'd left the ball last night had felt like an hour, an eternity. All I wanted was to be home, with her in my bed and with the world far away.

"Did you murder my niece?"

The question was abrupt, but in a way, not unexpected. I knew what people thought of me, what Esther must have heard about me. In fact, I was almost grateful that she simply came out and asked, rather than letting her unspoken suspicions poison things between us.

"No, I didn't kill Violet," I said, looking her in the eye. "We were unhappy. And I was not the best husband I could have been to her because of that. But I didn't kill her. The constables saw fit not—"

"We both know the constables would have thought twice before charging a man like you with murder, Mr. Markham," Esther said coolly. "So I don't care what they saw fit to do. But I do care if you are a dangerous man. Because as much as I've tried to persuade Ivy away from you, I see now that it's likely to fail. And I need to know that she's safe with you."

"Let me make one thing clear," I said, uncrossing my legs and

43

leaning forward, pinning her with my eyes. "I am indeed a dangerous man. I am in no way safe. But I belong to Ivy Leavold as much as she belongs to me, and I will never, ever let any harm come to her."

Esther swallowed, and I relaxed a bit, knowing the effect my direct stare often had on people.

"I didn't kill Violet," I repeated. "And while propriety and personal inclination force me not to name the circumstances, Ivy is aware of my alibi for that night and is satisfied of my innocence."

"I see," Esther said slowly.

I appraised her dispassionately, how her breathing had grown rapid and how she seemed unable to take her eyes off me. She responded to me in the same way Ivy had responded to me the first night I'd met her. *Esther's one of us*, I thought. *She just doesn't know it yet.*

Hell if I'd be the one to bring her into the fold—there was only one woman who could satisfy me now. But it may prove useful in winning back Ivy. Maybe she should come to the Baron's party after all. The Baron himself was quite a fan of breaking in the newly converted—or those who didn't even know they were converted yet.

"Miss Ivy Leavold," a servant announced, startling Esther. I stood, turning, and as always, feeling my breath catch. Christ, this woman was beautiful.

She wore a blue dress—some sort of pale color that set off her rich skin and glossy dark hair. That hair was bound up high, exposing the long elegant neck that I so loved to kiss, revealing the curve of her shoulders. For a moment, I lost myself in remembering what it felt like to push those shoulders down until she was kneeling in front of me. What it felt like to slide my cock past those soft lips . . .

I forced myself away from those perfect memories and stepped forward to kiss her hand. I didn't let my lips linger on her skin, but from the shiver that passed through her at my touch, I knew I didn't need to. I straightened and looked her in the eye. "Wildcat," I whispered.

A wistful smile ghosted across her lips. "Julian," she murmured.

God, what she did to me when she called me that. She had no idea, I knew. But she was the only woman who'd ever called me by my name—the only woman I'd ever allowed to call me by my name. To other women, I had always been Mr. Markham or Jules or any other number of variations—which I all encouraged. Let them think that informality and nicknames let them claim some sort of familiarity with me. They were wrong. But there was something so intimate about hearing my given name from Ivy's lips. Like she knew *me*. The real me. The real Julian.

Esther coughed politely and the moment dissolved.

"How about a stroll through Hyde Park?" I suggested, already reaching for Ivy's hand again. "It's a lovely day outside."

Ivy quirked her head at me, that smile still tugging at her lips, and I knew she was wondering what I was doing, what Julian Markham cared about taking a chaperoned walk through the park, why I was settling for chaste touches when we both knew that I'd rather have her on all fours panting in ecstasy.

It's all for you, I wanted to tell her as I pressed my lips to her hand once more. *Only for you.*

IVY

The day was unseasonably warm and incredibly windy, the trees heavy with leaves about to turn, but I didn't pay attention to anything other than Julian's arm, ever so casually brushing against mine as we walked. Esther trailed behind us by several feet to give us privacy. I wasn't sure what had transpired between her and Mr. Markham before I came downstairs, but Esther's attitude toward Mr. Markham seemed quite altered.

She had been very unhappy this morning when I told her that he would visit, but now . . . now she almost seemed to be encouraging us to spend time together.

"You look tired, Miss Leavold," Mr. Markham said. "Are you feeling well?"

I looked up at him. His tie was knotted neatly around his neck and his face was freshly shaved. So different from the half-wild appearance he often had at Markham Hall. He was so perfectly handsome right now, but yet, I missed that wildness, I realized. This was how a man should look and should act when he was wooing a woman, but I wanted more. I craved more. I needed it.

And then I shook my head, trying to clear that thought away. *No. Just because you need something doesn't mean it's right.*

But I couldn't keep myself from saying, "I'm feeling better now that you're with me."

His eyes fairly smoldered then, and his hands twitched, as if he were holding himself back from something. From fucking me, probably, knowing him. The thought made me grin.

"I like seeing you smile, Ivy," he said. "I wish I knew what was in that wild mind of yours."

A gust of wind blew through the park before I could answer, blowing leaves off the branches, surrounding us in a miniature storm of emerald green. I stopped walking and closed my eyes, lifting my face to the sky.

I felt the kiss of the air on my face, the brush of leaves against my shoulders and arms, and I wished more than anything I was back in the forest behind Markham Hall. I wished I was fresh from splashing in the stream or gathering flowers.

I wished I was home.

And then there was the whisper of rough fingertips on my cheek. When I opened my eyes, I saw Mr. Markham staring at me, lips parted slightly.

When he spoke, his voice was hoarse. "You have a leaf in your hair."

I laughed, but his face remained completely serious as he reached up and gently tugged it from my hair. And rather than drop it on the ground, he slid it into the pocket inside his jacket, the one close to his heart.

"Are you keeping that?" I asked teasingly.

Again, he stayed serious. "Until the end of time. Or until I can keep *you* instead."

Something twisted inside me then, something sharp, and I couldn't bring myself to examine it head-on. I didn't need to. I already knew what it was. It was love and it was pain and it was the realization that I wanted nothing more than to be with Mr. Markham and he wanted nothing more than to be with me and that it was only my fear keeping us apart.

But I couldn't just abandon my wariness, my urge to bolt and run at the sign of slightest trouble. I'd grown up with that wariness and it was more than second nature. It was my first nature.

I turned back toward the house without saying anything, keeping my eyes studiously on the ground. Why did he have to be so tender? Why did he have to be so perfectly *him*? It made this so much harder.

When we got to the front door, I turned back to him. Standing on the steps as I was, I had the rare opportunity of being taller than Mr. Markham. From here, I could see the rare strand of silver mixed in with his dark hair, and I could see how the sunlight caught on his long eyelashes when he looked up at me.

I wanted to say *I love you, come inside the house.* I wanted to say *I need you, I want to marry you.* But I couldn't without betraying the hours of anguished thought I'd given this very matter. What did it matter if I loved him, if the Ivy Leavold that loved him was just as toxic and damaged as he was?

"I'm tired," I said instead. It wasn't a lie. I was suddenly exhausted, and sleep was the only thing that sounded good. "I need to lie down. But thank you for your visit, Mr. Markham."

He didn't frown. He didn't scowl or protest. Instead, he

merely kissed my hand once more. "I hope you get the rest you need," he said, peering up at me from under his eyelashes. "And may I call on you tomorrow?"

I hesitated. I should say no, I should, I should, I should . . .

"It would make me very happy if you did."

CHAPTER 6

JULIAN

"*W*here's your valet?"

I was knotting my own tie in the mirror, taking care to make sure the silk lay perfectly flat against the high starched collar of my shirt. "I sent him out for more blue-bells," I said, stepping back to double-check my handiwork. "And I'm quite capable of dressing myself. I hardly used him at home anyway."

"Yes, but you looked like Robinson Crusoe at your home, Jules. Don't deny it."

I shrugged. What reason did I have for dressing up at Markham Hall? It was usually only me, and even after Ivy arrived, I was too preoccupied with her to make sure that my cravats were perfectly tied or my face closely shaven.

"Maybe if you didn't have such a taciturn valet, you'd use him more."

"Gareth's not that taciturn," I said, fastening my pocket watch to my vest. "He can be very cheerful." Although if I admitted it, he'd been anything but since we'd come to London. In fact, I'd go so far as to say that he'd been moody—for him—going many hours without speaking and disappearing at random intervals throughout the day.

But we had a slightly more complicated master-servant relationship than most, thanks to Violet, and so I didn't feel the need to castigate him about his attitude. And what did it matter anyway? Mrs. Brightmore and my cook, Wispel, had frankly deplorable demeanors but were competent and dependable. That's all I truly required.

"Are you ready?" Silas asked. "Any longer and I'm going to die of old age."

"Shut up," I said kindly.

I had decided to bring Silas along because I thought it might allay the fear I saw sparking in Ivy's eyes yesterday. Things had been too intimate between us, even without sex, and I could see the moment it spooked her. Silas had a way of easing people, of making any visit friendly and light, and besides, I wanted someone to distract Esther if I needed a moment of private conversation.

There was a rap on the door and Gareth arrived with my bluebells.

"Hello, sir," he said quietly. And to Silas: "Sir."

Gareth didn't smile or make small talk as he helped me pin the flowers to my lapel. I studied his face discreetly, wondering if he was so quiet because we were once again in London, where we'd both met Violet for the first time.

That must be it. And of course, he wouldn't feel right talking about it.

"Take the afternoon and evening off," I said impulsively, reaching for my wallet. I gave him a few pounds. "I'll be occupied all evening anyway, no sense in you waiting around."

"Thank you, sir," he mumbled. And with a shallow bow, he left the room.

Silas gave me a dramatic eye roll, and we made for the door, where there was a second knock.

"We're never leaving this room, are we?" Silas muttered, turning away. I opened the door to a hotel employee. "Yes?"

He handed me a note. "A woman asked that this be delivered to you, sir."

I took it, excitement surging in my chest. Had Ivy come? Perhaps she couldn't wait for my visit this afternoon and took it upon herself to come to me . . .

But when I unfolded the note, it wasn't Ivy's sprawling handwriting that greeted me, but a cramped and precise penmanship that nevertheless seemed familiar, though I couldn't place it.

Please meet me at the Serpentine bridge at noon tomorrow. Alone. Please make sure you are not followed by anyone.

-B

"Secret admirer?" Silas asked.

I flipped the paper over, looking for any other clues as to who it came from. "Did you see the woman who delivered it?" I asked.

The hotel clerk shook his head.

I truly had no idea who it could be. There was a time in my life when I would have suspected a variety of women, but certainly not in the past year, when I'd dedicated my life to Violet and then to Ivy. I tossed the note on the writing desk and gestured to Silas. "I'll worry about it later. Let's go."

* * *

"Have you given any thought to the Baron's party?"

We were strolling in the park once more, Ivy and me in front, Silas and Esther in back. Silas had worked his usual magic, and Esther was giggling and flushing like a girl half her age, and more importantly, giving Ivy and myself quite a lot of space.

"I have," she said, in that distant way that meant her mind was only half on our conversation. Her eyes were tracing the trees and flitting over to the Serpentine, where laughing people rowed small boats around the lake, and I knew she wanted to be doing more than pacing sedately through the park, taking part in the slow and dull parade of fashionable people trying their best to get other fashionable people to notice them.

I wondered if she noticed how they stared at her as we walked, admiring her, feeling jealous of her, looking so effortlessly beautiful in the smart striped gown that Esther had purchased. But no, she was oblivious to their stares, to the way the women appraised and the men gazed appreciatively.

"I'm not sure yet," she said. "About the party. If I belong there."

"Oh, you belong there, wildcat. The question is: will you *let* yourself belong there?"

She frowned, a tiny crease forming in between her brows. I wanted to kiss it so badly that I forced myself to look away to the lake, worried that my control would finally snap and that I'd have her pinned against a tree with my cock grinding against her while I devoured her mouth.

What I wouldn't give to have her legs around my waist right now . . .

I discreetly adjusted myself, forcing myself to think ice water and porridge thoughts while she looked off in the distance. She finally spoke, softly. "I'm afraid. I'm afraid of what I'll do if I go."

"I know."

"Ladies shouldn't want the things you make me want."

I stopped walking and so did she. "I didn't know that you were so preoccupied with being a proper lady."

She shook her head. "That's not what I meant. Not *proper* ladies but any lady. Any person. Do you think it's natural to want pain with pleasure? Do you think it's natural to want to be swallowed up by another person? No human with a free mind and working conscience should consent to those things."

"And why is that, wildcat? Do you measure your worth by how you love? Do you measure your humanity by the power you hold over people in love or the power that people hold over you in love? Who is anyone to say *this is right* or *this is natural*? Doesn't the very fact that you want it make it natural to you?"

"I . . . I don't know."

I took her chin in my hand and tilted her face to mine. "I think you do. Fear is part of this world, Ivy. So is uncertainty. But those things are only bad if they stifle us and keep us from living our lives the way we need."

She met my eyes, and her gaze was uncertain. "I'm not certain of anything anymore, Julian. The only thing I'm sure of is that I am still in love with you and that I don't know if that's a good thing or not."

She's still in love with me. My stomach knotted. How could there be so much love and *still* we were apart?

I couldn't help myself; I moved my thumb over her lower lip. It was so full, so soft, and then her mouth parted ever so slightly, and I grew instantly, painfully hard.

I'm not sure what my face revealed, but Ivy's pupils dilated as she looked at me. "I can't seem to make myself stop wanting you," she said huskily.

God, this woman destroyed me. It made me want to destroy her back—tweak her nipples and bite her clit and spank her ass for making me so in love with her.

"You know that you own me, Ivy Leavold. Let me prove it. Let me prove it for the rest of our lives."

A familiar flush crept up her neck, blossomed high on her cheeks. "I wish you would prove it here. Right now."

Christ. Did she know how close to the edge she was walking? It was only the frailest strand of self-control that kept me from pushing her down and rutting into her right here in the grass.

Instead, I leaned closer. "Do you really? How would I do that?"

Her breathing was faster now. "Maybe with a kiss."

"What kind of kiss, wildcat?" I was so close to her face now, my lips inches from hers. "Something chaste and contained, maybe. I could brush my lips once against yours and then pull away so quickly you'd wonder if it happened at all." I moved my face incrementally closer to hers. "Or maybe I could open my mouth just enough to taste you. Is that what you would like?"

She didn't answer, but her eyes were searching mine almost frantically now, begging me.

"Or maybe you want me to take your mouth like I used to. Without asking. Without playing. Maybe you want me to kiss you so hard that you can't breathe and you need me to hold you upright. Maybe you want to remember what it feels like to have me pressed against you, what it feels like to have me inside of you."

She was trembling now. "Please. Please kiss me."

I hovered there for a moment, so close that I could almost taste her delicious lips. But then I pulled back. This was so close to our usual rhythm—me steering, me controlling, and then relishing how she never gave in without a fight. But if she was to come back to me, it needed to be wholly and completely.

It needed to be willingly.

And so it was up to her to make the first move. Yes, I could kiss her and she would melt against me. But if it wasn't bolstered by her own free will, by her own choice, then no ground would be gained. She had to come to me.

So I pulled away from her face, watching the anticipation fade into disappointment, which then faded into a suppressed look of longing.

She looked away, blinking fast. "You're making me feel foolish. You're making me beg, out here, in front of everyone."

"No, wildcat. I'm respecting your wishes. Remember? You told me that I make it so that everything feels right when we're together, and then you are riddled with doubt after. I want to kiss you. Christ, I want to do more than kiss you—I want to fuck you until you can't walk and then bring you back home. I want to marry you. I want to watch your belly swell with my children.

But I love you too much to take those things—I want you to give them."

She was shaking her head vehemently, as if disagreeing. "But I'm asking you to take them."

"Are you? Or do you want me to take them so that you don't have to choose?"

"I—I don't—" But then she cut off, seemingly unable to give me the answer I wanted.

I smiled ruefully. "See? You're not ready."

She hesitated, then shook her head. No, she wasn't ready.

I touched her lips one last time. "But I think that, deep down, you want to be, don't you? Ready to marry me? Ready for me to be your teacher once again?" My voice turned into a growl. "You want to be ready for me to punish you again."

Her eyes fluttered closed. "Yes," she said. "Yes, I want to be."

I wanted to stand there forever, feeling her lips against my fingers and letting her words roll through me. But Silas and Esther had almost caught up to us, and even though I didn't care, I knew that people were staring at Ivy and me as we played this intense game of ours.

I dropped my hand. "It's getting late into the afternoon," I said. "Perhaps we should head back."

* * *

IVY

The smart white house on Eaton Place was a popular destination that next morning. After Esther's carriage stopped in front, having just pushed its way through the interminably slow traffic around Belgrave Square, I exited the cab and found myself in a swarm of suits and cigar fumes. There was a cacophony of muttered pardons and cleared throats and half-hearted offers to help me up the stairs, but I managed to dodge all of them and reach the front door, where I rang the bell.

I was bade to sit in the front room while the butler went to inquire if the mistress was available. As I did whenever I was trapped indoors and participating in an empty social ritual, I fantasized about running away. Simply disappearing and avoiding all of the subtle pits and traps of polite conversation, finding some more useful and productive way to occupy my time. But this morning was different. This morning I had woken up with Mr. Markham's words still looping in my mind, and I knew that he was right. He was right about my preconceived notions of what was natural and what wasn't, and he was right about my needing to be ready.

I had realized, as I had tried to go back to sleep, that what I wanted more than anything was somebody to talk honestly to about all this. I wanted to lay all of my fears and ecstasies in front of someone and not have them gasp in scandalized shock. Of course, this eliminated most of the people I knew. Esther was out of the question, not the least because I didn't want to shatter her fledging respect for Mr. Markham by telling her about some of his more particular tastes.

There was always Silas, but although I knew he would be able to comfort me and convince me that all would be well if I went back to Mr. Markham, that wasn't necessarily what I wanted today. Today I wanted honesty. I wanted the truth with all its cold surfaces and serrated edges. I wanted someone who had loved Julian Markham and lived to tell the tale.

Which was why I was at the London residence of Molly O'Flaherty, a woman I'd met at the same time I'd met Silas this summer. She was also a former lover of Mr. Markham's, and even though I knew they were no longer together, part of me was still fantastically jealous of her.

As if summoned by my envy, she appeared in the doorway, talking to a man as she walked in. "And send a letter to Gibbs straight away. If the board makes a move, it won't be without every lawyer in the city knowing about it. Hello, Ivy."

I knew that it would be appropriate to stand and drop a small curtsy, but Molly and I were beyond that. Beyond being falsely courteous to each other. She seemed to think so as well, because after dismissing her servant, she sank into the chair across from me without so much as a handshake.

"Why are you here?" she asked bluntly.

"I wanted to talk."

She rolled her eyes. "Of course you did. Is it about Mr. Markham? No, don't answer, of course it is." She leaned back in the chair, and the change in light revealed the redness lining her eyelids. *She's been crying*, I realized. I hadn't thought Molly was capable of tears, but when I looked at her closely, I could see the way her nose was chafed, as if by repeated swiping with a handkerchief. I could see the way her sapphire gown had uncharacteristic wrinkles in the silk, as if she'd been wringing her skirt under a desk or a table where no one could see.

It wasn't my place to say anything, but she really did seem upset. "Is everything okay?"

I expected her to snap at me or to ignore me. Who was I, after all, to ask her about her life? It had been clear to me since this summer that we would never be friends.

But to my surprise, she answered honestly. "No. No, nothing is okay."

She stood and walked over to a low credenza, where she unstoppered a decanter of whiskey. The habit was so like Mr. Markham's that I felt another pang of jealousy. They were such a good match in so many ways . . .

She poured herself a glass and then poured one for me without asking. She handed it to me and then sat back down. "The board of my company is trying to force me to marry."

"Why?"

"Fuck if I know," she said, taking a practiced sip of her drink. "I suppose they think that they'll have more luck controlling me if I have a husband who's on the board as well."

"I was under the impression that your company was doing quite well under your leadership."

"It is," she said fiercely. "It's doing more than well. But that's not enough for those vampires. They want more, more, *more*, and at a human cost I am not willing to deliver on. They forget that I am the daughter of a dock-worker before he worked his way up, and I refuse to pay those men a penny less than what they're worth. As a consequence, we have a workforce of strong, experienced, and loyal employees. If they think they can threaten me into submission, if they think they can come into my home and demand I take the yoke of some man so I'll be more *docile* . . . " Her voice shook with barely repressed anger and she turned her head away. But not enough that I couldn't see a tear well over and spill down her cheek. She ignored it, letting it fall into her glass.

I flashed back to the men pouring out of her front door. "They were the men outside."

"Yes, they were," she said bitterly. "They've all banded together, apparently, in some last ditch effort to 'bring me under control.' They plan to sell their shares and abandon the company if I don't fall in line."

"But surely they don't want to do that—the company is so profitable. I imagine it would be hard to walk away."

"Yes, which is why they are trying to force me into capitulating instead of leaving. They want to stay. But they want me neutered if they do." She was silent for a moment, then burst out, "God, I wish I could haul them back in here and wring their necks!"

I didn't know what to say. There was no comfort to be offered, really, nothing that I could say that would be something she hadn't thought of on her own. But I felt like it would be rude not to address her agitation. So I offered my honest observation. "You seem like the type of woman who gets what she wants. I have no doubt that you'll get the best of them. Somehow."

"Somehow," she repeated, staring at the window past my head. And then her eyes refocused, regaining their usual acuity.

"And I'm quite sorry to have confessed all this to you. You don't have any stake in this mess, and it's apparent to me that you don't care—and you don't need to care because we're not exactly friends, are we?"

I frowned. I did care, actually, in some strange way. Maybe Molly wasn't a friend, maybe I would always be jealous of her past with Julian, but she was in my sphere and I didn't wish her anything but success. And there was something satisfying about seeing another woman wrestle her way into the world of men with nothing but sheer force of will.

"Regardless," she said, "I do feel a peculiar kinship to you right now. It's Julian, I suppose, but perhaps it's more than that. You also seem like the type of woman who gets what she wants, although maybe you don't know it yet. Perhaps we are both cut from the same cloth."

"That's actually why I came to visit," I said. "I need to know if I am. Cut from the same cloth, that is."

Molly finished her drink and set her glass on the table. Artfully looping curls trailed along the silk shoulder of her dress. "And how exactly do you think I can help you?"

I couldn't think of a response to that because I didn't know. Coming here, all I'd held in my mind was the vague impression of Molly's confidence, her surety, the way she didn't seem to carry any guilt or shame about being the kind of woman preachers railed against on cold Sunday mornings.

I wanted to know how she could fuck so freely, how she could let herself be fucked in all the ways she wanted, without worrying about being subsumed by the darkness that seemed to accompany these tides of lust. It was hardly the topic for polite conversation, but I didn't have it in me to equivocate or dissemble. So again, I chose honesty.

"I love Julian," I said. "I love everything about him. His thoughts, his company, even his fits of melancholy. And I love the way he fucks me. But you know what he's like. He's . . . "

"Dark?" Molly supplied. "Overwhelming? Volcanic? Excruciating? Consum—"

"Yes," I cut her off. "All of those things."

"Sorry," she said and then examined her fingernails. "I've had a lot of time to think about it."

"But the thing is that I love that too. I *need* it. He's . . . " I hesitated, but then forged ahead—if there was one woman who wouldn't be shocked by this, it was Molly. " . . . he's done things to me that should frighten me. He's pinned me down and fucked me, he's pushed me, he's chased me, he's done things to me that I've never even known were possible—and I have loved every minute of it. Even the worst thing he's done, the very worst thing . . . in my secret moments, it arouses me. It makes me wish I had been there. Tell me that's not sick. Tell me I'm not twisted."

She cocked her head, letting her eyes slide slowly to mine. "You are sick, Ivy Leavold," she said. "Sick with something that doesn't have a cure. Of course, most of us don't want a cure, so there's that."

"But how do you live with it? Aren't you afraid of what you're capable of? Of what you'd let someone be capable of doing to you?"

She laughed. "Afraid? No. I promised myself as a child that I would not feel fear as a grown woman, and I have not. But, my dear, you and I are two different breeds of the same species. Do you think that Silas fucks the same way Julian does?"

I knew for a fact that he didn't, actually. My cheeks warmed, thinking of the three of us that night in York.

"It's the same with you and me. I quite enjoy the feeling of having power over a man. But I don't like being dominated and I refuse to feel afraid. You, darling, are the opposite. You want that fear. You want to have someone that you can surrender some part of your life to. Perhaps it's because you had no one to take care of you growing up, or perhaps it was encoded in your cells from birth. What does it matter?" She shook those perfect

60

copper curls. "You are too smart to want that surrender in all parts of your life; you don't want to be some meek hausfrau that faints whenever someone mentions the pollination of flowers. You want to have your life and your mind to yourself. But you still need the surrender, don't you? So what's a woman to do?"

She answered her own question. "You find a man who matches your needs. A man who will cherish you tenderly, who will respect you in all ways, but will insist that somewhere, somehow, in some part of your life, you totally and wholly capitulate to him. And you've found him. I've never seen a man so besotted as Julian is with you. He wasn't even this way with Violet. He will give you everything you need."

"But who am I who needs such things?" Tears choked my voice now, and I wasn't sure why I was suddenly so upset, but I was and I couldn't hide it. "I don't know if I like this woman."

"You don't have to like her," Molly said, standing. "You *are* her. You keep waiting for some epiphany, but the epiphany is the moment you realize that you don't need one. Face it: you are this way—whether born or made, it makes no difference. It's who you were meant to be. Imagine that you finally succeed in alienating Julian. That you never see him or anyone like him ever again. What happens then? You marry some man who cannot even begin to please you, or even *know* the real you, and you spend the rest of your days desperately unhappy—"

I was already shaking my head. No, no, I would never marry. Not if it wasn't to Julian.

She continued as if she hadn't seen my response, "Or you spend the rest of your days alone, also unhappy, and for what? For who? Who will be so rewarded by your denying yourself that it could make such an existence worthwhile? *You* will not be rewarded, because you will only be half a self, a husk. Society will not care—if you married Jules, that would be good enough for them. You think that by nursing these doubts you are some kind of saint? What does God care about how you like to be fucked? David lay with Jonathan, Solomon had concubines upon concubines, think of Hagar, Rahab and Tamar, and yet all of these people contributed to the ultimate action of God's will. False holiness will get you nowhere in life. But living it with those you love, following your heart—that is how you become the self you want to be. Now, if you'll excuse me, I have a business to run and a board to punish. Have a pleasant afternoon."

CHAPTER 7

JULIAN

*T*he day was chilly and wet, and a low layer of fog hung over the Serpentine. I leaned across the bridge, thinking a thousand thoughts—mostly having to do with Ivy naked—and so I didn't see my summoner until she was next to me.

"Mr. Markham," she said curtly.

I could barely hide my surprise. It was my housekeeper. My *housekeeper* of all people.

"Brightmore, what the hell are you doing in London?" *And not at my house doing your job?* I pressed down this last thought. It was the kind of thing that my father would have said, and I usually tried my best to be as different from him as humanly possible.

"First of all," she said, "have you been followed?"

"I don't believe so." I cast a glance around me, frowning. "And why does it matter? Brightmore, this is really most irregular—"

"I know it is," she interrupted. "Which is why I'll be as brief as possible. But I couldn't wait any longer to speak with you about this, especially if you bring another bride home."

God, I hoped I did.

"See, I realized—" Her voice stopped.

"Mrs. Brightmore," Gareth said from behind me. "Mr. Markham. Hello."

I ignored him and gestured for her to keep going. But she pressed her mouth shut.

"Sir, Mr. Cecil-Coke is looking for you," Gareth said. "He is ready to visit Miss Leavold."

"Of course." I looked at Brightmore. "Would you like to finish?"

She shook her head brusquely. "We can discuss the household accounts later, Mr. Markham. And I will continue with my shopping for new upholstery."

Household accounts? Upholstery? But then she gave me a sharp look and Gareth an even sharper one. Sparks, as if from metal grinding on metal, seemed to flash between the two of them, sparks of dislike or even hatred. For whatever reason, she didn't want him to know she was here. And while I disapproved—of her sudden presence here in London, of her need for secrecy, of the animosity between my valet and my housekeeper, I also trusted her. She'd been loyal and discreet the entire time she'd worked for me. I had no reason to doubt her now.

I gave her the slightest of nods. Brightmore turned on her heel and left, her solid footsteps reverberating throughout the bridge.

"Most unusual for Mrs. Brightmore to be here in London," Gareth remarked casually as we walked back to the hotel.

I kept my voice authoritative as I lied. "I asked her to come down to London to examine new fabrics for Markham Hall. If I do indeed bring Miss Leavold back home, I want her to be living among nothing but the best."

"I see," he said, although suspicion still laced his words. I turned to examine him.

"Is everything all right, Gareth? You've seemed distant lately."

"Everything is fine," he said. "Or at least in a few days it will be."

"Good."

And I didn't say anything more because I was going to see Ivy today and that was all that mattered.

* * *

THE NEXT TWO days passed in a quiet blur. Ivy was subdued and pensive when I visited, but yet, more receptive to me somehow. She let me run my fingers over her hand when her aunt wasn't looking, and yesterday, when I politely made my goodbyes and left, she caught up to me in the street.

I don't know what I'd expected—a kiss, a slap—anything was possible with Ivy Leavold. But instead she'd slid her hand into my jacket, her fingertips running over the soft cotton of my shirt, running from my chest down to my abdomen. My stomach had tightened involuntarily, and I knew that if she kept touching me, no matter how innocuous it actually was, I would probably do something we both regretted. I had been growing harder by the second, all of me so starved for her touch, and then she'd lifted her fingers and reached into the pocket inside my jacket. She'd pulled out the leaf I had put there earlier this week.

"You really did keep it," she'd whispered.

"I mean the things I say, Ivy."

She'd nodded then, as if hearing confirmation of something she already knew, and then replaced the leaf. When she'd turned to leave, I'd caught her hand.

"Are you coming to the party tomorrow?"

"I think . . . " She smiled at me and it was like watching the sun come out from behind the clouds. "I think I would like to."

"I'll be waiting." And then I'd kissed her hand and let her go.

And so, with these quiet advances in my mission, it was the

day of what I considered the final test. The day of the party. I knew that if Ivy came, she was mine, that I would finally be able to claim her for once and for all. And I had every reason to believe that she would come . . . so why was I so anxious?

"You are giving me a headache," Silas complained as we rolled toward the Baron's mansion outside the city. "She'll be there."

"I think so too. But what if she isn't? What if I lose her forever?"

"Well, you can't change it if you do lose her. As you kept reminding her, it's her choice. Therefore: out of your hands. Now relax and have a good time. If she doesn't show, you know that every woman and some of the men in that house would give their eyeteeth to go to bed with you."

"I'm not going to bed with anyone besides Ivy," I growled.

"Relax. I was joking. No one wants to sleep with you anyway. They'll be too busy sleeping with me."

I didn't respond, but I stared stonily out of the carriage window.

"Did your housekeeper ever find you again?"

I shook my head. Brightmore had left a note this morning for me to meet her tonight, again at the Serpentine, but there was no way I could miss the chance to meet Ivy, no matter what Brightmore had to say. "I asked Gareth to stay at the hotel, so he'll come get me if she needs something urgently. Otherwise, whatever she has to tell me can wait until tomorrow."

"I always thought there was a screw loose with her."

"There's nothing wrong with her," I said tightly. "Or my valet. Or anyone else in my life."

"Christ, you are tense today. You need a good fuck, Jules, or barring that, a stiff drink."

I rubbed my eyes with the heels of my hands. "I'm sorry. You've done nothing wrong, and I shouldn't be taking these things out on you."

"I'm used to your brooding, old boy. Now you better put your mask on. You know how the Baron gets."

* * *

IVY

I brought Esther to the Baron's. It may not have been wise, but I didn't see how I could hide it from her, short of sneaking out of the house, and I wasn't ready to do that. Not when I was so uncertain about tonight as it was.

Besides, when I mentioned that I had an invitation to the most exclusive party in Britain, she showed nothing but unfettered glee. She had even insisted that we shop that very day for masks, and she wouldn't stop talking about how *shocking* she heard it all was, and also how delighted she was to go.

"But you mustn't gossip about what you see," I'd reminded her firmly. "The people at the party wish to protect their identity, I'm sure."

"Oh darling, I'm not planning on gossiping. I'm planning on *participating*."

A surprised giggle had forced its way out of me. "Esther!"

She'd given me a look. "Being an old spinster like me confers certain privileges, you know. And being wealthy. No future bridegroom of mine would ever fuss about unstained sheets on our wedding night. Now, do you want the Persephone mask or the Aphrodite mask?"

But even having Esther with me wasn't enough to quell the nervousness bubbling in my chest. Ever since talking with Molly, I'd known I was ready to choose, ready to go back to the man I loved. But I knew him and I knew myself, and I would be lying to myself if I pretended that tonight wouldn't test my limits, physically and emotionally. Because he was my teacher, and I his pupil, and he had proven over and over again that he took our roles very seriously.

There would be punishment. There would be discipline.

And I was wet just thinking about it.

"Ivy, stop fidgeting. You're making me nervous."

"Sorry," I said and she patted my knee affectionately.

Gravendon House was lit up magnificently as our carriage approached, gas lamps mingled with torches along the gravel drive, every window limned with golden light. When the wheels stopped, Esther bustled quickly out of the carriage, eager to get inside, but I waited a moment. I could hear the music and laughter from out here, and I wondered if one of those laughing voices was Mr. Markham's. I wondered how I would feel riding home in this carriage tonight, after the party, or if I would indeed even ride in it. Perhaps I would go home with Mr. Markham.

"Ivy, come on! It's freezing out here."

I crawled out of the carriage, forced to accept help from the footman due to the voluminous dress my aunt had forced me into, and joined her, making sure my Persephone mask was still tightly tied around my head. Esther smiled at me, and together we walked up to the door.

Inside, it was just as loud and as bright as I'd expected. People laughed and danced, servants milled, and every corner was awash in bright colors, in gold and silver, in flashing jewels and gleaming glass. The guests and the house seemed one and the same, melded together by their vibrancy and wealth, and the two were inseparable to me as we walked farther inside. These happy faces, these expensive silks, these large mirrors and these glittering chandeliers—it all seemed like a dream, too vivid to take in, too fantastic to believe. A fairy world that emerged only at certain twilight times, only to evanesce and vanish in the face of day.

A man stood near the stairs, marked by his scarlet sash and air of authority, and I surmised he must be the Baron. He was a tall man, with very broad shoulders and a very narrow waist—an athletic frame. A strong frame. He didn't seem to be any older than Mr. Markham, but so much power and raw, classical masculinity rolled off him that one could not doubt he was experienced. With money, with lovers, with life.

He came towards us at once, and part of me wanted to step back, to bolt and run, rather than have to talk to this man, but Esther strode right up, all curves and satin and dangling blond curls. She looked beautiful, and the Baron did not miss it. He took Esther's hand and kissed it, letting his gaze linger, and even with the mask, I could see the blush creeping up Esther's face.

"I don't believe I've had the pleasure," he murmured.

"I'm Esther Leavold," she said. "I'm accompanying my niece, Ivy."

At my name, his eyes flickered with interest. "So this is the Ivy Leavold that has Julian Markham so taken?"

Now it was my turn to blush. Did Mr. Markham really talk about me so often that my name was known to one of the peers of the realm? Or was it Silas who had told him?

Either way, I could no longer hide. I stepped forward and gave a small curtsy.

He turned his attention back to my aunt. "And you are the woman from Bombay who has arrived with a massive fortune and no husband."

Perhaps it hadn't been Mr. Markham or Silas who'd told him about me. Perhaps the Right Honorable Lord Gravendon was simply one of those people who knew everything.

Esther was smiling at him now, all pink lips and white teeth, and I watched as the Baron stared at her mouth. "Yes, no husband. I haven't met a man suitable enough yet, and besides, if I were married, I would miss the chance to chaperone Ivy to such exciting events."

The Baron's voice was low when he spoke. "Now, Esther, I hope you will give your niece a few unchaperoned moments? To reunite with her fiancé?" His brown eyes were boring into hers with a heat that was palpable even to me.

"Of course," she said faintly.

"Turn around for me, Esther," he ordered abruptly, his voice graveled.

Blushing and clearly surprised, Esther obeyed, spinning a slow circle while he watched, his pupils dilating.

"Might I claim the pleasure of your company for part of the evening?" No one missed how his voice rolled over the word *pleasure*. "Since you are a new guest, I would very much enjoy giving you a tour of the house and introducing you to my friends."

"I would be honored," she stammered. I'd never heard Esther stammer before.

He leaned down and whispered something in her ear, and she laughed her tinkling laugh. Then she turned to me. "Go on, dear, it's all right. Go find him."

I didn't wait to be told twice.

The party swirled and undulated around me, a sea of champagne glasses and feathered masks, and it was all so decadently gorgeous, so dreamlike. But what struck me as I walked toward the ballroom was not how out of place I felt, but how perfectly at home I was with it all. I was at one with this vision, I belonged here. I wasn't shocked by the couples kissing openly on the dance floor, I wasn't scandalized by the shirtless man—still masked—being chased by a group of similarly masked women. People pressed close together, in various states of undress, so that there were flashes of creamy white skin as the other dancers spun and stepped as if there was nothing different here than at the London assembly halls. The smell of wine and sex hung in the air as thickly as the trilling notes from the eight-piece band in the corner, and men and women licked their lips and beckoned to me as I passed, and I collected it all inside of me, pieces of a jigsaw puzzle that was my new life.

How could I stay away from this? This state of ripe and unfettered sensuality, where wildness was not a condition to be tamped down and pruned away, but something to be celebrated and admired?

I passed by faces I knew—Molly, Silas, Helene, Adella, Gideon. I evaded their grasps and crooned invitations for now, only wanting one person. The person I came here for.

And there he was, standing by the far wall, leaning against the paneling and looking bored. He had on a simple mask of black cloth tied around his face, with two openings for his eyes, and even with his impeccably tailored suit and a silk tie that probably cost more than anything I'd ever owned before I met him, he looked roguish and untrustworthy. A pirate or a high-wayman, an outlaw ready to commit another crime.

And, oh, how I wanted that crime to be committed against me.

CHAPTER 8

JULIAN

I felt Ivy's eyes on me. I don't know how, across a ballroom of that size, and where admittedly a fair number of people had been looking at me all evening. But I felt it in the prickling heat on the back of my neck, in the way my body suddenly lurched into hyper-awareness, the way the mask felt against my face, the way the fabric of my clothes moved against my skin as I turned. Why my pulse pounded, I didn't know, because she had told me she was coming tonight. I had expected it, prepared for it, but still—the enormous, wonderful, almost stupidly joyful truth of it was so much more than I had anticipated.

She was really here. She'd come back to me.

The ballroom was sunken two or three steps from the main floor, and she stood at the top step, her dark eyes pinned on me. My dick surged just seeing her; she looked beautiful in the way that only Ivy managed to pull off—both incredibly fuckable and unbelievably ethereal at the same time. Her gold silk dress was sleeveless, so I could trace the lean curves of her shoulders and

72

collarbone right to the low bodice, where her breasts strained against her corset. I wanted to suck on them until she begged for me to fuck her. I wanted to press them together and slide my cock into them. I wanted to cup them as I took her from behind.

She came towards me then, descending the steps, and I stayed where I was. Every atom of my body screamed to go to her, to meet her and catch her up in my arms, to wrap myself around her and never let go, but I had already waited so long for her and I had to be sure. Had to be sure that she really wanted this, wanted me. Because after tonight, I wasn't letting her walk away again. I couldn't. It would kill me.

She seemed oblivious to the stares of the other guests as she passed through the crowd, but I wasn't. As always, the sting of jealousy only heightened my arousal, my need to reaffirm that she was *mine* in all the ways that counted. They may fantasize about that long dark hair—tonight curled up so elaborately and studded with diamond pins—but only I got to twist it around my fingers as she sucked on my cock. They may stare at the slim lines of her torso, but only I got to hold her down and come on her flat stomach as she lay panting from the orgasm I'd given her.

Mine mine mine.

And that's what I said when she reached me. When she lifted her eyes to mine, her face half obscured by a delicate black and white mask, I couldn't restrain myself any longer and I yanked her roughly to me. "Mine," I whispered in her ear.

"Yours," she murmured.

And then she did something that nearly shredded me. She laid her head against my shoulder and sighed happily. It was like having a bird land willingly on your finger or having a tiger purr under your touch. It was both magical and humbling.

"Christ, Ivy," I said, my voice growing unexpectedly rough. "You're really here." I turned my face into her hair, smelling that scent that was uniquely hers—soap and flowers and something like rain—and breathed it in, wanting to spend my entire life with her in my lungs, in my blood.

"You were right," she said, not moving her head. "You were right all along. I'm so sorry."

I tucked my finger under her chin and lifted her face to mine. "You never have to apologize to me. Do you understand?" Her eyes searched mine as I spoke. "If you hadn't left, you would've always wondered what would've happened if you had. You would have always had one hand on the door, and this way, we both know. We both know that you came back, on your own."

"I feel like I've wasted so much time. Being away from you. Being away from myself." A tear welled and then slid under her mask to trail down her cheek.

I wiped it away with my thumb. "I was desperate without you and I was furious that you hurt yourself." I licked the tear off my thumb, wanting to lick more of those tears, wanting her to know that every single one belonged to me. "Because your heart is mine, wildcat. You betrayed and wounded yourself and you suffered, and it's my job to protect you from suffering."

"I'm sorry," she whispered, eyes downcast.

I leaned forward to nip at the shell of her ear. "You're here now. That's what matters."

She pressed against me, running a hand up my chest to cradle the back of my neck, and she pulled me down to her lips. I groaned the moment our mouths touched, unable to keep myself from grinding my erection into her corseted stomach. Her lips were so warm, so soft, and I devoured them, my hands sliding down to grip her upper arms as I moved my mouth over hers, parting our lips so I could taste her.

She tasted exactly like I remembered—perfect.

I had wanted to wait to make love to her the first time; I had wanted to bring her upstairs to a soft bed and take my time worshipping every inch of her body before I moved on to her punishment, but I had to be inside of her right now, and there was no way I could wait. Luckily, at the Baron's, I didn't have to.

"Follow me," I said, taking her hand and pulling her behind me. I led her to a wide velvet bench obscured by a curtained alcove in the far corner of the ballroom. I sat and she followed, but I wrapped my hands around her waist and lifted her so that she was sitting sideways in my lap.

"Come here," I growled, pulling her flush against me as I pressed my mouth against hers.

She made small sounds in the back of her throat as we kissed, kittenish noises of pleasure, and then gasped when my hand found the inside of her ankle. I continued moving up, her skirts hiding most of the activity, finding where her stockings ended, tied with delicate silk garters. And then there was nothing separating me from her pussy. Which was gloriously, perfectly wet.

She squirmed, trying to grind against my hand, and I pulled it back, amused. "So greedy, wildcat."

"It's been so long," she said. "I need you."

"Right here?"

"Right here."

My cock was as hard as stone, thick and pulsing, and even if it hadn't already been my plan, there would have been no way I could deny her. "Hold on," I said, subtly rearranging her skirt so that her bare ass and pussy rested against my trousers but still hid everything from view. I reached underneath her and fumbled with my buttons, my hands shaking from too much desire, too much excitement, too much suppressed need. Even the stimulation of freeing my shaft was enough to make me close my eyes. Fuck. I wouldn't last long at this rate.

"Hurry," Ivy said, wriggling deliciously in my lap. "Hurry."

With my dick free, I held the base as I guided her to a semi-standing position facing the ballroom. Her cunt hovered a few inches over me, and I could feel the heat of her, making my balls tighten in anticipation. Then I guided her down.

From the outside, our movements had been so incremental that it must have looked like she'd merely adjusted herself on my lap. Improper, of course, in a normal setting, but nothing to look twice at here. But what they couldn't see—what even I couldn't see but could only feel—was the wet silk of her kissing the head of my cock and then slowly, slowly working its way down. Each centimeter—each and every millimeter—felt tighter and hotter and wetter than the last, each perfect inch a reminder of the heaven I'd held so briefly in my hands and let slip through my fingers because of my own shadowed past.

But now, as she finally seated herself and as I tilted my hips up and guided her legs farther apart so that I was truly sunk to the hilt, I could really believe that my heaven had returned. Ivy Leavold was mine once more.

And now that she was here, now that I was once again feeling her wet cunt stroke me, every rough fantasy and every wish for untempered dominance over her returned with a vengeance. I had to push away the thoughts that crowded my mind just then —images of her ass pink from being spanked, of her eyes blindfolded and her mouth open for me. Of tying her to a table and letting every person here caress and lick her until she was too exhausted to come anymore.

I bracketed her waist with my hands, my fingers digging into her corset with the restraint it took to stay still and let her work herself on me with tiny, imperceptible movements. I buried my face against her silk-covered back, resisting the urge to take control.

"I want more," Ivy whispered after a moment.

"We can go upstairs."

She paused and then angled her body so she could look at my face. I inhaled sharply at the sudden twisting, biting the inside of my mouth to keep from coming right there and then.

"That would be nice," she finally said. "But I didn't necessarily mean . . . "

She struggled with her thoughts. "It's not about where we are necessarily. It's just—well—the last time I left you, you punished me. Do you remember?"

Did she really think I could forget? I had relived every

moment of that day thousands of times, from the moment I'd discovered that she'd left—impetuously, without money or a plan—from the moment I came in her ass. Like the day we'd spent traveling to York, I'd woken up the next morning with a sore cock, but it had been beyond worth it. I shuddered now, unable to keep myself from vividly recalling the feeling of sliding into her tight entrance, the way her body shook as she came.

"I remember."

"Well . . . " she hesitated then forged ahead. "I thought you would punish me tonight."

I stiffened and my hard cock grew—impossibly—harder. "Do you *want* to be punished, wildcat? Right now?"

She turned some more in my lap, sideways now, still impaled on me. "Yes," she whispered. "I want you to discipline me, like you did on that day. I know now that I need that. I need that from you. I want to prove to you tonight that I am ready to commit to you—to us—with all of me."

God, I loved her so much. I loved her so much that the word *love* seemed ridiculously inadequate for the magnitude of what I felt. I wanted to cut myself open and make her crawl inside of me. I wanted to live and breathe and drink every moment with her, for her, and then die for her a thousand and one times.

I leaned my head against her shoulder, trying to fight past the emotion closing my throat so I could speak. "You are perfect," I told her, my voice low and choked. "You are so perfect and I don't deserve you."

She pressed a hand against my cheek. "Julian."

All she needed to say was my name, and I felt as if she had uttered a wedding vow. I moved my head so that I could bite her, none too gently, on her bare upper arm. She gasped, tightening involuntarily around my member, and I savored the alarm that flashed briefly in her eyes.

"Are you sure you want to do this? You might be afraid of me."

"I want to be afraid of you, Julian. I want you to try to break me, and then I want you to catch me and put me back together. We'll have plenty of time for things that are slow and tender, but tonight . . . "

"Your wish is my command," I said, lifting her off me, hiding the wince that came with losing the perfection of her pussy wrapped around my shaft.

The darkness had already flooded my mind at that point, my fingers itching with the need to tie knots and pull hair, every muscle in my body primed to fuck. And then I would fill her with my seed, pump her so full that she'd be dripping with it for days.

Mine.

* * *

IVY

The party had progressed while Julian and I had been in our corner, and now there was even more evidence of the hedonism that the Baron's house was so famous for. As I stood and rearranged my skirts, I watched as a dancing couple moved over to a table and the woman was unceremoniously bent over and fucked by her partner. Men and women were kneeling or being kneeled to, and noises of pleasure—sighs, groans, the unique sound of slick flesh—now vied with the music and laughter for prominence.

Julian only had eyes for me, however, and he grabbed my upper arm and jerked me out of the alcove, his fingers digging into my bicep. He'd buttoned his trousers, but it did little to hide the magnificent erection bulging there, although he didn't seem to care—or notice as people stared at it hungrily.

I assumed we were going upstairs, but he stopped me at the ballroom steps, making me stand on the lowest one while he stayed on the ballroom floor. The extra six inches meant that I was now exactly at his height, able to stare into his emerald eyes and see the wicked intent glinting there. A trickle of fear triggered a flood of lust. Yes. I was doing the right thing. This is what I wanted.

"Raise your skirts, Ivy," he ordered, the tortured tenderness from earlier gone. He was the teacher once again, commanding and stern. My whole body surged with want at that sternness.

I obeyed him, lifting my skirts to my knees, exposing my silk stockings.

"To your waist," he corrected me.

A crowd was starting to gather around us, drunk guests, sober guests, all watching the legendary Julian Markham finally bring his wayward fiancée to heel. I gathered that somehow we were the main event, that Julian was important among them, and that they were tacitly invited to my subjugation.

This was hard. I'd forgotten how hard it was to obey sometimes. But I did it, hoping that the silk and lace hid my trembling as I raised my skirts higher, knowing that my naked sex was now visible to the crowd.

There were murmurs, but Julian ignored them as he once again freed his thick organ. With one hand wrapped around himself and his other arm seizing me around the waist, he pulled me close and entered me in one rough thrust. We'd never fucked like this before, and the angle was new and strange and I needed a minute to adjust—

But there was no time to adjust because then he took my leg and slung it over his arm, widening his access to me and also exposing even more of me to the crowd. He slid in and out with long, sure strokes, keeping me balanced as he showed everyone in the ballroom to whom I belonged.

"Do you see them watching you?" he said in a low voice as he continued to fuck me. "They're watching your pussy stroke my cock. They're watching your tits push against your dress. They want to fuck you too. They want to pass you around and take turns with you, to mark you like property."

I moaned. It was a thought I would never entertain in my right mind, but I wasn't in my right mind, not with that thick cock stroking me with its slow, inexorable strokes, and right now, I would consent to anything. If Mr. Markham willed it, I would let myself be taken by this crowd of strangers and I would come on cock after cock, all while he watched.

"Lucky for you, I'm too jealous a man," he said. "But perhaps...other mouths? Other hands?"

The crowd surrounded us now, and I hadn't realized that Helene and Adella were behind me, until I heard Adella's melodic Gallic accent as she told me to hold still. I turned to see what was happening, and then I realized that the girls were undressing me, tugging my dress off my body, and then Mr. Markham pulled out of me, leaving me empty and wanting, but there was no way I could protest because then he was kissing my mouth as they continued to strip me out of my clothes.

Mr. Markham unknotted his tie as he kissed me, and then he pulled back so that Helene could tug at the ribbon holding my mask in place. I hadn't realized how protected it had made me feel, having my face partially shielded from view, but once it was gone, I felt more exposed than ever, even though I was already next to naked.

My corset went last, and so I stood in my stockings, my hair still perfectly coiffed, feeling the cool air kiss the wet skin between my thighs. I knew that everyone could see my arousal. I only hoped that *everyone* didn't include my poor aunt, but the thought evanesced as soon as it came, irrelevant, unwanted. My only job, my one task, was to be right here, doing Mr. Markham's bidding. I didn't have to worry about anything else, because I knew that he would take care of me. He would make sure I was safe.

He wound his tie around his hand and unwound it, his jaw tight as he surveyed me. "Now it's time to pray to be forgiven," he said, unwinding the length of silk for the last time. "Now it's time to show me how contrite you can really be." He stepped backward, clearing a space for me on the ballroom floor. I followed him.

"Kneel, wildcat."

I knelt.

He walked behind me and then the silk tie rasped over my skin, settling with a cool weight over my eyes and the bridge of my nose. The world went completely dark as it was tied tightly at the back of my head. I heard him walking around me, examining me, and then his low baritone as he was in front of me once more.

"Open your mouth."

I did as I was told, parting my lips in welcome. He ran his thumb over my bottom lip, then pulled it down so my mouth was open even wider.

I was given no warning, no hint, when he abruptly pushed into my mouth, all the way to the back of my throat. I willed myself to relax, not to gag, as he moved in and out. I could taste myself on him, smell our clandestine intimacy on his skin, and when I thought about how it must look—me, naked and blindfolded and kneeling, and him, masked and thrusting into my mouth, I grew almost desperate with the need for . . . for something. It was to be fucked, yes, but it was also to fuck, to give pleasure as well as receive it, and nothing sounded more delicious than making Julian come with my mouth and my tongue. I loved the noises he made when he was close, the way his stiff cock grew even larger in that potent, intoxicating moment right before he released. I always felt like a goddess then; like in the end, he had been the one to surrender somehow, even though it was me who was bound and exposed.

I bobbed my head faster, flattening my tongue against him, and I was rewarded by his hands threading through my hair and pulling it hard as he took control and started fucking my mouth with a ruthless, almost cruel pace. I heard one, two, three hairpins drop to the marble floor as he twined his fingers tighter and tighter around my tresses, and I also heard the breathless whispers and sex noises of the crowd around us.

And just as I thought he was careening over the edge, when I was sure that he would drive into my mouth one final time and erupt, he was gone—his cock out of my mouth, his hands off my head. He'd been almost holding me up by my hair and so I fell forward onto my hands, on all fours now.

Julian bent down and whispered in my ear. "I've been saving myself for you, Ivy. When I come, I'm not wasting it on your mouth. When I come, I want to be deep inside of you and I want your pussy tight and swollen around me then. So let's get that cunt ready for me, shall we?"

"It's ready now," I said. I tried to rise up on my knees but was pushed back down. His hand was warm against the center of my back, pressing down on the spot in between my shoulder blades and running along the curve of my back. I froze when it reached my tailbone and it stopped for a minute, and then he trailed a deliberate track down to my quivering cunt. My cunt, which everybody could see.

His voice went even quieter. "Does this embarrass you, wildcat? Does it humiliate you?"

I nodded.

"Then why are you so wet?" His fingers danced over my drenched folds, prodding and pressing.

"You know why," I whispered.

"Yes, I do know."

And then he smacked my ass so hard I saw stars.

CHAPTER 9

JULIAN

J'd planned on testing Ivy's limits tonight, but I was the one being tested right now. I had almost come in her sweet mouth, and God, I had wanted to. Seeing her blindfolded like that, on her knees and waiting with her lips open at my command . . . and then feeling the eyes of the crowd on us as I relentlessly fucked her mouth . . .

But even though I knew I'd be able to get hard as many times as I wanted—Ivy had that effect on me—I wanted to suffer alongside her. Since I was making her endure my discipline, I would endure along with her, and I would make sure that I didn't release until she'd been thoroughly sated. Until I'd made up for all the time we'd lost. Until her body well and truly remembered its master.

It was not easy.

Like right now. She was on all fours, her knees spread apart so that her glistening cunt was free for anybody to see. It took all of my willpower to keep from kneeling behind her and sliding inside. But I didn't. Instead, I raised my hand back and slapped her ass, the sound cracking through the ballroom like a whip. I stood up, my erection tugging at every nerve in my pelvis, and turned to Silas.

"The dining room," he said calmly. He was as gifted at self-control as I was, although for a different reason. I used self-discipline as a method to satisfy my whims—by controlling myself, I almost always got what I wanted at the end. Silas simply didn't know how to be anything but polite and jovial, even when he was coming all over a woman's face.

I nodded my agreement. And then I bent down so Ivy could hear me clearly. "You may stand now."

She obeyed, getting to her feet, her legs shaking slightly. Her nipples were tight jeweled points and there was a blush high in her cheeks. It wouldn't be long after I let the others touch her that she would come.

I took her hand in mine and led her past the observers in the direction of the dining room. Some followed, some returned to what they had been doing, entertained by the spectacle but not intrigued enough to participate. I didn't care. It didn't matter if there were two hands on Ivy or two thousand, I would still make sure that every iota of pleasure was wrung from her body tonight.

She followed me almost meekly, the blindfold inhibiting her normally confident steps, and I was careful to steer my wildcat around obstacles and people, stopping only when we reached the dining room. Dominated by a massive table, the dining room was empty of guests and food, the table completely cleared of the remnants of supper.

"I'm going to pick you up and lay you down," I told her. She nodded, looking so sweetly confused and eager that I couldn't help but kiss her right then, letting my lips linger on hers. Then I lifted her easily and laid her on the table.

The cold wood against her back and legs sent goose bumps racing over her skin, and I watched them hungrily, wanting to lick her pebbled flesh, to bite it. She looked perfect like this, her breasts round globes, her back arched in such a way that I could slide my hand under her lower back without ever touching her skin.

There were twenty or thirty people around the table now, and I recognized every face among them. Most of them were good friends, some were acquaintances, but all were people I'd trust to touch my pet. The Baron didn't allow cruelty or selfishness in his house, and as a result, he'd cultivated a set of people who both flouted the sensibilities of the outside world but respected individual boundaries. But still, I felt like I needed to clarify.

"Tonight, my fiancée has returned to me," I told them. I put a hand on Ivy's bare stomach, loving how the soft flesh trembled underneath my fingertips. "And I am so happy." Stupidly, my words cracked, and I swallowed the emotion back down. "But tonight, I remind her who she belongs to. Does anyone have something I can bind her with?"

Rhoda and Zona, the blonde twins, both hastily unfastened their silk sashes, and Silas offered up his tie. With their help, soon I had Ivy's legs tied to the bottom corners of the table and her right arm to the top. I turned to look for another sash or tie, and found Lord Gravendon standing behind me, quietly offering his own cravat.

I gave him a smile in thanks and then finished tying Ivy to the table. The position of her arms above her head made her breasts jut higher and her back arch more. Her legs were spread farther apart, and from here, I could catch the barest glimpse of her rosy seam, just begging to be fucked.

"You may touch and kiss as much as you'd like," I told the guests. "I only ask that I be the only one to fuck her."

And then I stepped back. As soon as my hand left her, she visibly tensed, and I knew this was something that both scared and secretly delighted her, the strangeness of having many mouths and hands on her, the vulnerability of being exposed and exhibited.

Silas was the first to step forward, with a wink at me, and then he leaned down and whispered briefly in her ear. I saw her relax the slightest bit. She trusted Silas; he was a known—and charmingly kind—quantity. He told her something else as his hand brushed lightly over her stiffened nipples and she gasped, squirming unconsciously toward the stimulation. Soon others came closer, caressing her limbs and dropping kisses on sensitive sections of flesh. Spikes of jealousy flashed through me, sending jolts of arousal straight to my groin. It was delicious torture, watching this, watching others tease her into arousal and then coax that arousal into climax. It made me feel violent and possessive and so very, very in love at the same time. It was like the pain and envy highlighted the lines and borders of my feelings for her, like a contrasting dye on fabric, making every sensation sharper and more vivid.

Ah, never mind. I couldn't even properly explain it to myself. Who could ever really explain the parameters of lust? Or what sparked arousal? By its very nature, it didn't make sense logically or empirically. It was something that spoke to the deepest parts of our minds and bodies, something that bypassed reason, societal mores, and even our sense of shame. All I knew was that I was ravenous with the desire to watch Ivy come on this table, and come hard.

"She's quite beautiful," the Baron murmured.

"She is," I agreed, watching her hands grip their ties as someone finally brushed against her pussy.

Gravendon put a hand on my shoulder. "I hope you've finally found happiness, Julian. You deserve it."

I looked at this man, my mentor in so many things. Though he was only older than me by a few years, he had already been completely settled and secure in his desires and practices when I met him as a young man, still reeling from Arabella's death. It was as if while the rest of us had to wrestle and realize and continually rediscover who we were, Gravendon had simply sprung from the ground fully formed, a muscled god of sex and power. He had found me, grieving and confused by these impulses that I couldn't control, and had shown me his world. It was then that I saw who I really was, what I couldn't deny myself being. He had helped shape me more than my parents.

I answered, "Yes, I think I finally have."

"Good." He said it warmly, with great affection. "And anyway, her aunt is asleep in my bed, and I would like that to be a repeat occurrence. So you're not allowed to alienate her niece." He smiled the smile of a man who'd just discovered a new treasure.

"You and Esther . . . " I had been right after all. She was one of us.

As if reading my thoughts, Gravendon said, "Yes. She's quite a treat. A natural submissive, a true submissive. I only have to speak and she can't help but to act." There was an uncharacteristic tenderness in his eyes that I rarely saw when he talked about his partners—generally the Baron only engaged in sex, not anything resembling emotional attachment. "She's never been properly taken care of before. She nearly cried with happiness afterward." He shook his head. "It was quite gratifying."

"Congratulations. That's quite a conquest."

"It was unexpected, to say the least. I plan on asking her to return. Or to stay." He looked over at Ivy, who was now panting. "May I?" he asked.

"Be my guest."

He smiled at the irony and walked over to the table. Ivy seemed to sense there was something different about his touch, because she froze as he moved a wide hand from her neck, down between her breasts, to her cunt, which he cupped hard.

She wriggled, trying to get closer, and he gave a small smirk. "She's greedy," he told me.

"Don't I know it."

He pushed a finger inside of her and then another. She jolted at the contact and then moaned as he started in earnest. I knew from many years of playing side by side with him that this was something he excelled at. I knew that in only a few moments, she'd be shaking and screaming.

And after she was finished, I was taking her upstairs. And making her mine once more.

* * *

IVY

"Do you feel that, wildcat? You have a peer of the realm touching you right now. He's going to make you come with the same hand that has written to princes and kings. He's going to fuck your hole with his fingers, and everybody is going to watch him do it."

Mr. Markham's voice was low in my ear, and his words were like a stimulant to my already over-stimulated body. There were mouths on my breasts, on my fingers and stomach, and then the hand that was on my pussy. It was the hottest, wickedest hand I'd ever felt, because it carried none of the tenderness or regard that always resonated in Julian's touch. It was selfish and demanding and I knew without a doubt that I was being touched only because it pleased this person to do so, not because he particularly cared about pleasing me.

And it was relentless; the pleasure it brought with it was sharp and sudden and almost uncomfortable. I tried to move away, but the bindings on my hands and feet made it impossible. The fingers slid in and then slid back out, the palm grinding against my clit as they did, in and out, in and out, over and over again until there was nothing but slickness and fire between my legs.

I could feel it building and building, and I began not to care how I looked or what I sounded like or what the people around me thought. I was caught up in the tide of pleasure, that peculiar release that only comes with surging past the waterline of humiliation. I was now shamelessly trying to grind my pussy into the man's hand, trying to arch my back to get even closer to the mouths on my breasts.

"That's it," Julian said. "Let them make you come. Let them see how sweet that body looks when it's coming."

"I'm—I'm going to," I managed, feeling the muscles in the soles of my feet cramp as my body twined tighter and tighter. "I'm going to come, oh God—"

And then I did, surging against my bonds as my core collapsed and exploded outward, mercilessly provoked by those demanding fingers between my legs, provoked into coming harder and longer and more fiercely than I thought my body could stand. And the people around me kept going, drawing still more waves and tremors from me, until finally I stopped struggling, unable to do anything but lay back and feel.

"Good girl," said Mr. Markham. "Very good."

And indeed, my pussy was given a rewarding stroke, much in the way one would affectionately caress a well-behaved animal.

"Now, another one."

"No," I said, trying pointlessly to roll away. "I can't, I can't—"

"I told you that we would get that cunt ready for me. Now because I'm nice, I'll make sure they use their mouths and not their hands. I can't have you too sore to come on my cock later."

Someone was climbing onto the table with me. "But—"

I stopped as I felt a warm mouth seal over my clitoris. The sensation right after orgasming was too much, too overwhelming, and I kept trying to squirm away, even though I knew I couldn't. And then, impossibly, there were two mouths, licking and licking and licking, moving in tandem so that there was never a pause, never a reprieve, and even though their tongues were soft, their mouths were hot and their fingers dug into the soft flesh of my ass. The overwhelming sensitivity was swallowed up by the new tide rushing through me, all the faster and stronger for the orgasm that came before it. Now I pulled at my bonds not to escape but to get closer. I didn't want to come on someone's tongue, I wanted to come on their cock or fingers.

Whoever was between my legs now, I wanted them to fuck me. I was beyond caring who did it now, but the thought of a stranger or Silas or the Baron fucking me right in front of Julian—and his ensuing jealousy and the punishment that would follow as he fucked away every trace of any other man—it sent me over the edge and I released again, crying out now, crying out for Julian and imagining his green eyes the entire time I came.

It was only as I floated back down that I realized the room was filled with noise. The normal sounds of a party—music and laughter and clinking glasses—and the sounds that were unique to Gravendon Manor. The low moans of a man being fucked, the sounds of clothes being shucked to the floor.

I was untied and then my blindfold was removed. I blinked at the sudden light, my pupils contracting painfully, and I was still blinking as Mr. Markham helped me sit up and then gathered me in his arms. His face was the first thing that came into focus, his bright eyes and his hungry mouth, and he looked all sorts of dangerous—angry even.

"What next?" I whispered, trying not to look at the people around us. I only wanted to see him now, I only wanted to feel him, and as always, I only felt hungry for more, not sated in the least.

"Now we go upstairs."

And without so much as a word to those around us, he picked me up and carried me away. I was still completely naked and he was still completely clothed, save for his cravat, which now lay crumpled on the floor, ignored. He carried me effortlessly, without strain, and I rested against him, wrapping my arms around his neck. As aroused as I still was, I could also rest like this forever, snuggled against the warm, strong chest of the man I loved.

I sighed happily.

He looked down at my head resting on his shoulder. I felt him swallow. "You're going to be the death of me, Ivy Leavold," he said, voice serious.

We reached the second floor, where it was much quieter than the first. As we walked down a hallway, towards a destination Mr. Markham seemed familiar with, unmistakable sounds came from the different doorways, and I knew beyond a doubt that these rooms were made for guests to play in. Julian confirmed this when he set me down to open a door at the very end of the hall, quite isolated from everything else.

Inside, the room was filled with things both familiar—a bed, a chaise, pillows, and a thick rug—and unfamiliar. Restraints mounted from the walls, floggers that looked like they were made for horses, flat wooden paddles.

"What is all this?" I asked, even though I had a good idea.

"The Baron has unconventional tastes," Julian said, locking the door behind us. "And he also likes to accommodate any potential whims of his guests. Look at me, Ivy."

I turned, not sure what to expect. Mr. Markham stepped forward, his eyes pinned on mine. "Are you ready?"

"I've been ready."

"Really? And are you scared?"

I thought about that thick erection hidden in his trousers. I thought about the selfish, possessive look on his face and all the times he'd pushed my body past the point of endurance.

I nodded. Yes. Yes, I was scared . . . and inflamed and so wet that I could feel it on my thighs.

He stepped forward again and his hands circled my neck, his thumbs meeting in the small crescent of my clavicle.

"You're not scared enough."

CHAPTER 10

JULIAN

I wanted to eat her, like a wolf in a fairy tale. I wanted to crush her to my chest until she was part of me, her atoms commingling with my atoms. I wanted to bend her, break her, and then watch her beg for more.

Maybe she was right. Maybe we were sick. But if that was the case, I never wanted to get better. I never wanted to be cured of *her*, her smell, her taste, the way the light caught in her silky hair. The way the soft flesh of her throat just gave and gave under my fingers. How could someone so strong, so fierce, be housed in a shell that was so frail?

"I could snap your neck right now," I murmured. "I could squeeze here—" I increased the strength of my grip just barely, only enough to impede her breathing the smallest bit, fascinated with how my fingers felt against the delicate inner workings of her throat—muscles, tendons, veins.

She gasped, her eyes flashing an amber brown, widening in fear. But she didn't step away, she didn't reach up to fight me, she didn't say *bluebell*. No, instead she relaxed into my grip, her eyes fluttering closed, her head lolling back as if she was offering even more of her throat to me.

I wanted this when I fucked her, I decided. I wanted that ultimate submission, that ultimate trust in her eyes and face when she came. I wanted it on her face when *I* came too, when I finally filled her.

That single image, that single concept of my hands on her throat while I came, it was enough to block my ability to think, to plan. I dropped my hands and she inhaled deeply, opening her eyes.

I took off my coat, letting my eyes rake over every inch of her naked body as I did. Now that we were completely alone, I had time to drink her in fully. Her full breasts, still tipped with hardened nipples. Her narrow waist that flared into athletic but still womanly hips. Those long lean thighs that I loved to feel around my neck . . .

I took off my shirt. "Bend over and grab your ankles."

She obeyed, but not before I saw the resistance flare in her eyes. God, how I loved that resistance. If I didn't leave this room covered in scratches and bitemarks, I'd be devastated. I wanted to know exactly what she was thinking, exactly what she was feeling at every moment, even if it was violent.

I walked around her, examining her like a purchaser might examine a piece of art he was interested in. Her hair was coming unbound, several curls brushing the floor. The line of her back was almost perfectly flat—Ivy was quite flexible. A shame that I hadn't exploited that properly before, but I assured myself I would plenty in the future, now that we had a future together. The happiness I felt at that thought made me pause to collect myself. She wanted this punishment and I needed to give it, and while I would give in to my joy as soon as we were finished here—give in to my urge to shower her with kisses and words of love—I needed to remain focused. I completed my circle, back behind her again, squatting so that I could chafe her taut calves while I examined her sex. It was visibly swollen now, and I slid a finger inside to test exactly how much.

Perfect.

I stood, looking down now, watching the rosebud entrance of her ass. Without warning, I slid the same finger inside there, making her tense. "Relax," I ordered. It took a minute, but I finally felt her muscles lose some of their tension. I rewarded her by grinding my covered erection against her pussy while I worked that finger.

"You know, wildcat, it wasn't in my plan for tonight, but I'm going to take your ass too. After I come in your pussy. You make me come so good with your ass. I think about it constantly."

She let out a little noise—a mewl—of pure desire. "Oh kitten," I whispered. "You're going to have to stop making noises like that or I am going to have to punish you even more just to hear them." With her bent over gripping her ankles, my finger in her ass and my dick pressed against her, if she so much as squeaked again, I was going to come without even unfastening my trousers.

Mastering myself, I stepped back and delivered a firm slap to the right side of her ass, loving the way she twitched but didn't let go of her ankles. I knew some people enjoyed paddles and whips and straps, but to me, the pleasure was in feeling her skin against mine, in personally smacking the ass that so brazenly tempted me even when it was hidden under skirts and petticoats.

I spanked her again and again, watching her ass glow and her muscles strain as she struggled not to lose balance. Strike after strike rippled through her flesh, and it wasn't long before I could see how she'd gotten even wetter, her pussy glistening with desire. I needed my cock there. I was beginning to lose track of everything else.

"Stand up, wildcat," I said finally, slightly out of breath.

She did and she didn't wait for any other instructions, but

grabbed my arms and pulled me close. "Fuck me, Julian," she begged. "Please. I can't take it anymore."

"Oh you can't?" My voice was close to a snarl now; I was at the edge of my control.

"You said—"

"Quiet," I ordered, and then—with a discreet glance to make sure we were by the pile of pillows—I shoved her down as roughly as I dared, wanting to lick every line of anger and fear that creased around her eyes and mouth. And before she could recover, I was on top of her, cruelly grinding my cock against her, the fabric of my trousers abrading us both, the friction both painful and amazing.

"Is this what you want?" I demanded, grinding harder.

Her legs fell open and she moaned.

"Tell me, wildcat, did you think about my cock while you were gone? Did you miss it? Did you try to make yourself come with your fingers in your cold bed? When you know deep down that you can only be satisfied by me?"

She nodded, her brown eyes limpid pools of pain and desire. "Please, Julian. If you don't fill me . . . " Her hands came up, as if she was trying to gesture the idea that she couldn't put into words, but that didn't work either.

My jaw clenched, thinking about that perfect cunt unattended for so long, thinking about the other people who had touched it tonight, thinking about what would have happened if I *had* lost her forever and some other man had gotten to fuck it whenever and wherever he wanted I slowly unbuttoned my trousers and let my cock free.

I ground against her again, now bare skin on bare skin, and she was so goddamn wet that I would slide right inside of her if I wasn't careful.

"Tell me you want it," I said hoarsely. "Tell me what my kitten wants."

Ivy was practically writhing underneath me now, her hands

everywhere—fisting my hair, sliding into my trousers to touch my ass. "Hard," she managed. "Break me."

I angled my hips and drove in so roughly that she cried out. All I could feel and think and know was that tight little pussy around my cock, that perfect pussy, my perfect wildcat, and I was gone, rutting like an animal into her, pounding her like a savage. Even so, my mind kept a tally of her reactions, her moans and sighs and fingers digging painfully into my ass—though I chased my own release, hers was paramount. I was doing this for her, and I never wanted to hurt her. At least, not in a way that she didn't enjoy.

But for the most part there was nothing but fucking. Copulating. Just bare primal need as I pistoned into her exposed snatch. But it wasn't enough. I needed more, more leverage, more power.

I got to my knees and hoisted her hips up to match my pelvis. There. *There.* I held her hips up, but I adjusted one hand so that my thumb rested on her clitoris, and I rubbed it in tight, controlled circles as I slammed into her over and over again.

"You're so tight, kitten, so wet and warm. I'm going to love coming inside of you. I'm going to come so hard."

Her eyes were almost completely closed now and she was making those small mewling noises again, high moans in the back of her throat that drove me fucking crazy. She was tightening around me, a flush gathered on her stomach, and I dropped her back on the floor, still working her clit, still thrusting into her. Yes, she was going to come, almost now, and I moved my hand up to her throat. The fear flashed in her eyes again, but then—deliciously, perfectly—she arched her shoulders and neck, offering herself up to me. I only pressed down enough to restrict the air just so that it was noticeable. And then carefully, and with the utmost control, I squeezed a little harder.

For the barest second. For one second where her eyes went wide and her mouth parted and then I let go.

She sucked in a deep breath, her eyes large, terrified orbs.

And then she came like a shot around me—harder than I'd ever felt her, harder and tighter, and Christ, I was there too.

"*Fuck*," I hissed, her cunt squeezing me like a vise, her body trembling as she cried out, and then I thrust into her one last time as brutally as I could, pumping her mindlessly like an animal, as a wave of heat exploded at the base of my spine and I came.

She continued to shudder around me as I growled and ground my way through this release, my vision going black at the edges. I could feel the liquid heat of my climax on my shaft as I continued to pump her full, and when it finally, finally abated and my vision cleared, we were both covered in sweat, panting as if we'd run a race. But it had been worth it.

"I love you, wildcat," I told her, wishing she could know how much and how truly I meant that. How I meant it on a cellular level. On a spiritual level.

She had gone completely limp, her eyes half open and her breathing finally slowing down. "I love you too, Julian."

I pulled out and rested back on my heels, keeping her legs spread with my hands. And yes, I saw what I wanted to see, and no matter how base or primally possessive it was, seeing my seed in her thrilled me.

Mine.

"On your stomach," I said, lowering her legs. "Now."

She did as she was told, but I could see from the careful way she moved that she was sore. Once she settled on the rug, I stroked her hair away from her neck and shoulders, so that I could drop kisses there later, and moved a pillow under her hips to angle her pelvis the way I wanted. I stood and gathered some supplies—the Baron's rooms were always well-stocked for any scenario—and then I returned to her, kneeling by her side.

I unpicked the silken knot of a garter, wanting her completely naked. Even though I'd just fucked her harder than I ever had, even though I'd forced her to disrobe in front of a house full of party guests, there was still something strangely intimate about pulling the garter free and peeling the stocking from her leg. I moved to the other side, repeating my actions, and then running a hand up her bare leg to her ass. I played with it for a minute, loving the firm but soft feeling of it under my fingers, loving the glimpses of her pussy as I squeezed and let go, squeezed and let go.

I uncapped a bottle of oil, drizzling it on her back and down her legs, and then I began to rub it into her skin, massaging and kneading every muscle in her body, from the ticklish soles of her feet to her swan-like neck. I massaged each and every finger, stopping at her left ring finger to kiss the spot where my ring should be . . . where it would be as soon as this was over. I massaged her scalp until she sighed with pleasure and closed her eyes. I massaged her until she went from limp to limper, until her breathing slowed into the slow draws of the nearly asleep.

Then I found another bottle of oil. Unlike some oils made for this purpose, it did not numb the user completely. In fact, the numbing agent was specifically designed to preserve as much sensation and enjoyment as possible while also taking away any bite of pain. The last time I had done this, I had wanted it to be rough. I had wanted it to not be easy and I had made her come anyway, come despite the pain and the fear, as a lesson to her. Although I would be lying if I said I didn't enjoy every second of fucking that luscious ass.

Tonight, though, tonight I wanted to pamper her like I had originally planned on. I wanted her to enjoy this and love it and want more. I wanted to show her that I could be kind too. That as much as I thought of bonds and begging and unshed tears, I also thought about kissing and caressing and the kind of sex that carried you from joy to joy like a bridge over a stream.

I bent down and licked her pussy, starting at her clit and ending at the small pucker I intended to bury myself in. She sucked in a breath as I flicked my tongue around, and she raised her ass up in the air mindlessly, unconsciously, her body begging for more.

She would get it. I used my finger to work the new oil in and out of her, as my other hand played over her cunt. The smell of crushed roses—the perfume of the oil—filled the room. Soon, her ass was so slick that it shone in the firelight, and I could tell the numbing effects of the oil were kicking in, because she was raising up against my finger even more now.

I added another finger, working her a bit more aggressively, watching her sex pulse with want. She was grinding her pussy into the pillow now, and I backed up to watch it, slathering the first oil on my dick as I did so. It was beautiful. A work of art. Her legs spread, her head down, tiny whimpers issuing from her mouth as she rubbed that needy cunt on the pillow, rubbed and rubbed, the whimpers growing louder.

I was fucking mesmerized. I had gone from lubricating myself to simply jacking off now, fisting my cock to the sight of her unabashed mindless need. God, I couldn't decide if I wanted to fuck her or just watch her, but then her hand slid under her stomach to her clit, and my brain stopped engaging in that particular dilemma. I had to come inside her again and that was all there was to it.

I lowered my body over hers, her ass pressing into my pelvis, and I began to bestow all the kisses I had promised myself I would earlier, letting my lips linger over the nape of her neck and in the delicate spot between her shoulder blades.

"I'm going to go slow," I promised her. "I want you to feel good."

She nodded, her eyes still closed, her fingers still working under her and then I positioned myself at her entrance. The oil did its job, because while she inhaled at my invasion, she didn't wince or shudder. Instead, she stayed relaxed as I pushed in, moaning as my weight pressed her clit harder into her hand and the pillow.

I slowly sunk in, using one hand to gentle and stroke Ivy as I did. I wanted her to know how much I worshipped her. I wanted her to feel every inch of my need for her. I wanted her to come while I was so deep inside of her that she couldn't tell where she ended and I began.

I slid out a little and then back in, burying myself as deeply as I could. She continued to moan and mewl and pant, and so I moved incrementally faster, my mind starting to fragment into single thoughts, staccato words.

Slick.

Wet.

Tight.

Jesus Christ, so fucking tight.

Ivy tensed underneath me, rocking her hips more and more, and I knew she was about to come again.

"Come for me, kitten," I said in her ear. "Let me feel it."

She cried out, and then I did feel it, the hot velvet of her clamping down around me.

Fuck.

Instead of thrusting harder, I wrapped my body around hers as she shivered her way through her climax, and I let her pulsing channel massage me into coming, the tension in my pelvis rising and rising, my body stoked into fire simply by being inside her. I didn't even have to properly fuck this woman, and she could still make me erupt, merely by being herself.

I groaned as my release stabbed through my balls and then my cock, and I shot into her, holding her tightly as I did, breathing against the back of her neck, one forearm under her breasts and the other under her stomach.

We lay like that for a long time, maybe hours, and when I finally rolled off of her, she was sleeping a pure, deep sleep that I couldn't bear to disturb. Instead, I went and found a blanket and two more pillows, arranged a makeshift bed for us, and fell asleep too, my body wrapped around hers once more.

* * *

IVY

I would dream about this night until my dying day, I knew. Nightmares of the thrilling feeling of his hand tightening on my throat—and then dreams of bliss of the moment he'd let go. Life-giving air had flooded into my lungs just as the most intense orgasm I'd ever felt had flooded through my body.

It had been so very Julian. Dangerous and erotic and addictive, and even as my eyes fluttered open to the weak rays of dawn and my thoughts flickered to my aunt, I wanted it again. I wanted it all again—the humiliation and the public fucking, the choking and then the sweet and gentle way he had made love to me in the end, all rose perfume and tender, infinitesimal movements.

But I would get to have it again, I realized as I opened my eyes all the way. We were reunited. We would be married. And nothing, *not anything,* could separate me from the man I loved again.

"You don't have to wake up, wildcat," Julian said. His voice was sleepy and rough, as though he'd just woken as well. "Let's stay here forever."

I snuggled into him, laying my head on his chest and listening to his steady heartbeat. He stroked my back in long, somnolent strokes. "Can we?" I asked, my eyelids already growing heavy.

"Yes," he said. "Whatever my wildcat wishes, she shall have."

"In that case, perhaps I wish that we were married. Today."

I was seized into a tight grip, crushed against his muscled chest. "Then your wish is my command."

I tilted my head back so I could look up at him. "And then we can go home?"

"And then we can go home." He moved his mouth to mine, kissing me so languorously, so deeply, that my toes were curling by the end of it.

A loud knock sounded at the door. Mr. Markham frowned.

"Stay here," he said, standing and tugging his trousers on. He didn't bother putting on a shirt.

He opened the door, and the room was flooded with lamplight. "Are you Julian Markham?" a voice asked.

I didn't like that voice. I didn't like it at all.

I sat, hoisting the covers up to cover my chest as I did, alarm beginning to drip thinly through my veins. Mr. Markham straightened. "Who is asking?"

"Inspector Glemwell, Scotland Yard. You are under arrest for the murder of Violet Leavold."

"The hell I am—"

Several men now entered the room and I couldn't see my lover. I stood, not caring what I looked like only wrapped in a blanket. "You can't take him!" I said. "They didn't charge him in Yorkshire and you can't charge him here—"

"New evidence has come to light," one of the constables told me matter-of-factly. "An arrest must be made."

The men were pushing Mr. Markham out of the door now, and I stepped forward, ready to claw and scratch him free if I had to. The constable who had talked to me grabbed my arm, and I struggled against him, trying to get to my master. My Julian.

"No," I said. "No!"

Julian twisted, every muscle in his stomach tensed, and his green eyes met mine. "I'll be back, Ivy. I promise. As soon as I can."

I shook my head, tears of shock and confusion threatening to spill. "No," I whispered. "You have to stay here with me."

"I promise I'm coming for you," he said, his eyes burning into mine as if he was trying to keep me safe from all this through sheer force of will. "And I always mean what I say."

And then he was gone.

After a minute, the constable left too, dropping my arm unceremoniously, and I went to the window, watching as the police and Mr. Markham left the house. I don't know what he had said to them on the way down to the ground floor, but they weren't holding him now, and he walked alone, ahead of them, shoulders as straight and broad as always. Even with the lack of proper clothes, with the trousers that hung low on his hips and his exposed chest and arms, he looked unbelievably powerful, unbelievably dangerous. A prince roused to war.

But even my prince couldn't win this war. And they had new evidence? What did that even mean? How could they have new evidence when I knew for a fact that he hadn't killed Violet?

But do you really know? an awful voice whispered to me. *Maybe you were wrong to trust him, to believe him.*

I leaned my head against the glass pane, shutting my eyes against my tears and the sight of the police carriage rolling away towards the center of London. No, I wouldn't let myself go there. I had made the decision to trust him. I had made the decision to come back to him. I would stand by those choices. No matter what new evidence the police claimed to have, I wouldn't let them plant new seeds of doubt in my mind. I knew what Mr. Markham's real sins were, and murder wasn't one of them.

But what did my believing in him ultimately do? What if he was charged and found guilty and imprisoned or—oh God —executed?

No. *No.* I wasn't doing that. I wasn't putting my thoughts on that path. I was going to get dressed and then I was going to find my aunt and then say goodbye to the Baron—

Of course! The Baron would know what to do. He was friends with Mr. Markham and a very influential man. If anyone could help, he could.

Someone in the army of discreet servants the Baron employed had brought up my dress from downstairs and laid it across the bed. I dressed as hurriedly as I could, my tears drying up as a plan formulated in my mind. I would enlist Lord Gravendon's help and then we would march down to the police station and end this madness. I was not going to lose Mr.

Markham after having just come back to him. I would not allow it.

There was another knock at the door, and I turned, for a moment expecting the police again or Mr. Markham or anyone other than Gareth, looking well-groomed and politely concerned.

"I know it's rude of me to barge in, Miss Leavold," he said, "but Mr. Markham has directed me to see you back to your aunt's house. He doesn't want you to be affected by this any more than necessary. And I think we should be quick—as soon as word spreads that he's been arrested, the newspaper men will be coming here and to his hotel and to your residence as well. We need to get you safely ensconced inside so that they can't harass you."

I looked out the window as I nodded. "Yes, yes. But let me find my aunt—"

"I've already spoken to her. She plans to stay here with the Baron, but she will come home this evening."

"And I need to speak with the Baron—"

"He already knows about the arrest," Gareth broke in gently. "He's already gathering together several powerful people in the government—peers and judges and lawyers. Mr. Markham won't be locked up for more than a few hours, I promise."

Everything had been taken care of. And in true Julian fashion, he had even found a way to take care of me in the meantime.

"Okay," I said, slipping into my shoes. "Let's go."

As I walked out, I grabbed the tuxedo jacket crumpled on the floor and pressed it to my face, breathing in the sun and soap smell of him, hoping it wouldn't have to substitute for the real thing for long.

CHAPTER 11

JULIAN

*T*hey spared me the indignity of handcuffs, but not the indignity of being forced into the police station itself. I frankly didn't care that I wasn't properly dressed—someone offered me an overcoat as I walked in, and I ignored it. But I did care that I was here, pointlessly.

I was more irritated than angry, more weary than worried. I had little doubt whatever "evidence" they had I could easily overrun. But it was at a cost I had avoided paying until now: telling the truth. The truth that the world would surely hear, and then my sins would be publicly laid bare. The world would know beyond a doubt how deep the veins of darkness ran in my soul and exactly how dense the ore of my transgressions was.

But as exhausting and peevish as that would be, I didn't really care about anything other than extricating myself from this encumbrance and getting back to my wildcat.

My wildcat who had wanted to get married this very day.

Let them know. Let them all know the awful, despicable

truth of it, and then let me get back to my life, which had finally become something worth living.

I was led to a chair near a wide rolltop desk, and I flung myself in it unceremoniously. "How long will this take?" I asked the inspector.

"You must be questioned," the inspector said, "and then processed. Then a formal—"

"There's no need for that," I said, using a tone I usually only unleashed on my enemies—or my rebellious wildcat. The inspector closed his mouth quickly, blinking. The tone normally had that effect. I continued. "We will discuss two things, right now. Firstly, you will tell me what this new evidence is and how you came by it. And then I will tell you what happened on the night of my wife's death. Then I will walk out of this station and you will carry on with more important matters."

"I don't—that's not—"

"Inspector, I suppose you realize that, at any moment, I could call an army of barristers, judges, and peers to my aid, do you not? We both know that I will not be in this station longer than a few hours, and you can spare yourself much embarrassment— and I can spare myself much trouble—if we both embrace this truth. Now. The evidence."

His mouth opened and closed a few times, and he shifted papers around his desk, shuffling handwritten files and letters, refusing to look at me.

I knew how he felt. I knew he didn't want to lose face in front of his men, and I knew that whatever evidence he thought he had must be pretty damn compelling, because he was obviously torn between complying with my reasonable suggestion and upholding the letter of the law. But even though I empathized with his conundrum, I was not in the mood to sacrifice my time and energy simply to accommodate a stranger's needs.

I put my hand on the table. I didn't say anything more, I

didn't touch him, I simply reminded him of my presence, and he sighed.

"Your manservant. Gareth White."

"What?"

"Your manservant gave us eyewitness testimony about you murdering your wife."

No. It wasn't true. It was a thousand times not true. For one thing, Gareth could not have eyewitness testimony of anything of the sort, because I didn't do it. While that saddle cinch was being cut, I had been balls deep in a clergyman's wife. And secondly, Gareth had been nothing but incredibly loyal to me his entire tenure—even if he had seen me commit a crime, I would have believed him to keep my secrets to the grave. He wouldn't go to the police with a true story, much less a false one.

Or would he?

After all, he had been in love with Violet and he must have known what I did to her that final night. I would be surprised if her shouted pleas and loud sobs hadn't reached every corner of the house. And I had not been quiet either—I didn't spare Violet one note of the pleasure I was revenging myself with. I wanted her to hear every groan and every sigh, every curse as my balls had tightened and I filled that Harold woman over and over again. It had been her anguish that made me hard, her emotional pain that had driven me to exorcise every single insult and injury she'd dealt me, exorcise them on a willing lover right in front of her.

Yes. Perhaps that was what drove Gareth to lie to the police about Violet's death. A quest of mistaken justice. Punished for the wrong thing, perhaps, but at least punished.

Would my sins always haunt me? Would I never be free? No. I didn't deserve to be free.

The inspector finally met my gaze. I kept it steady and cold, even as a tumult surged in my mind, and I said, "Thank you. Now shall you like to hear my version of events?"

* * *

Two hours later, I left the police station, again without the overcoat, ignoring the stares of the passers-by on the sidewalk. A smartly appointed carriage waited in the road for me and the Baron opened the door from the inside as I approached. I got in.

"I knew you could take care of yourself," he said, lighting a cigarette.

"But you were waiting outside just the same."

He shrugged. "I like to look out for my flock."

I smiled at that. "The Church of Gravendon."

"Indeed. Were you forced to tell them the truth? Silas hinted at something quite salacious last night but didn't go into details."

"He's a good friend." I leaned back, the leather seat cold against the bare skin of my back. "I told them the entire story and directed them to contact Mrs. Harold of Stokeleigh and Silas Cecil-Coke of Coke Manor with their inquiries about my alibi. I doubt they will; the inspector seemed painfully embarrassed by the entire tale. But the option is there, if they need further satisfaction that I'm innocent."

"Which they shouldn't. I wish I would have been able to prevent all this, Julian, but I didn't know they were even there until you were being dragged out. But believe me, I would have stopped them."

"I know."

"At least you managed to see to your pet. I would have taken care of her, you know, but I do know how you like to personally oversee things."

I had been looking out of the window, staring at the busy streets and the dull iron of the autumn sky, so it took a minute for me to process what I'd heard. "See to my pet? Ivy? I assumed she would be safe with you—"

"And she would have been. But I am not criticizing, Markham, merely pointing out a fact. It's perfectly natural that you arranged for her to be taken to her aunt's."

I was so confused. "But I didn't arrange it. There wasn't any time—and besides, it wasn't necessary. Like I said, I knew Ivy would be safe with you."

The Baron narrowed his eyes. "Your valet took her away. Why would he do that, if not on your express command?"

Gareth. Gareth had Ivy.

The Baron must have seen something in my face. "What is it?"

"We have to find her. Now."

* * *

IVY

What was Mr. Markham doing now, I wondered. How was he feeling? Apprehensive? Angry? Determined?

I knew he would keep his promise. In my lap, I held his tuxedo jacket, and there was that leaf, now paper thin and brittle, nestled inside the chest pocket.

I always mean the things I say.

I glanced away from the jacket in my hands and up to the window. We'd taken a cab home to Esther's, although the trip from Gravendon House was taking much longer than I remembered it being last night. Outside the window, I saw only unfamiliar things—low brick buildings and wet docklands. Esther didn't live anywhere near here.

"Do you think we're lost?"

Gareth looked up to me, his blue eyes glinting in the dark. "I think we're going exactly where we need to go."

"I guess . . . "

He was over to my side of the cab in an instant, something in his hands. Something that gave off a sweet smell. Nothing about this gesture or the accompanying prop made sense to me, and I half wondered if I was dozing right now, dreaming some impossible dream.

He leaned forward, his hand coming to rest on the cab wall behind my head, and I pressed against the wall, trying to give myself space, worried for an insane second that he was going to kiss me. "Gareth, what are you—" I was cut off by a large cloth being forced over my face.

What the hell is happening?

I twisted and kicked, feeling my shoe connect with his thigh, then again with his knee. With monstrous strength, he held the cloth fast and I knew from reading the cheap novels Thomas so abhorred that there was something in the cloth, and that I must not breathe it in if I could help it. So I held my breath and went limp, sagging against the seat as if whatever potency that was in the cloth had taken effect. As I watched through my mostly closed eyes, Gareth relaxed his grip ever so slightly, and that's when I knew I had to act. Any longer and I *would* pass out, so it had to be now.

I reached up with one hand and dug my thumb into his eyeball, and he fought me off. It was the distraction I'd hoped for, directing all his attention upwards while my hand moved downwards. And with a swiftness sped by prayer more than skill, I found the soft package between his legs, squeezed and twisted that worthless package as hard and as far as I could.

Gareth screamed and the cloth fell away, and even though it was a terrible idea, the prey animal in my mind couldn't stomach the thought of not bolting, not running, and I opened the cab door and flung myself onto the street.

I tried to land on my feet, but my ankle bent sharply to the side. I cried out, falling onto my hip and hands, and I saw the cab screech to a halt, the puzzled cab driver standing on his perch and trying to figure out what just happened.

I had a choice. I could trust this man, this stranger, who was three feet away from my would-be kidnapper and possibly paid by him or I could run.

I was Ivy Leavold. Of course, I chose to run.

Pain stabbed through my ankle as I hitched up my heavy silk

skirts and ran through the docklands, but I didn't let the pain in. I didn't let the panic in or the questions or anything—my brain only registered the need to run and so I did. I was good at running. I was fast. I was strong. I was born to move. Pinning me down—capturing me—was like trying to make the Thames flow backwards, it was like trying to hold the wind in your hands.

This was what I'd been born to do and I was going to be safe.

The docklands were not very busy—we were much farther upstream than the thriving docks on the East End—but there were people in sight, within an easy running distance. A boat-yard, it looked like, and on the road, even farther down, carriages. I was going to be safe I was going to be safe *I was going to be safe*—

Something hit me from behind, hit me hard, and all the breath left my body as I went pitching forward into the muddy ground.

I couldn't breathe and there was something on top of me and I couldn't move either . . .

"I wanted this to be easy for you," Gareth said. "I wanted it to be so easy."

And this time when the cloth came, I couldn't fight it. I squirmed and tried to roll and tried to hold my breath, but it was impossible. And when I finally relented and inhaled, I could feel the substance leaching the fight from my limbs, the will from my mind. My eyelids started to close of their own accord, and everything began to spin away, distant and distorted, like the world through a magnifying glass tilted at the wrong angle.

And then: nothing.

* * *

HEAVINESS CLUNG TO ME. A thick drowsiness. A sopping wet blanket of disorientation and dizziness.

I was in a sitting room. A very nice sitting room, although

SIERRA SIMONE

the furniture was covered in sheets and the portraits were taken down from the walls.

I was not at the docklands. I was in a house.

I couldn't lift my head, but I knew without looking that it was now early afternoon. And I knew that I was on a chair, my hands bound behind my back and I knew that I wasn't alone.

"Why?" I mumbled, struggling to make my mouth move. My lips felt numb, my tongue felt fat. But that one question crystallized in my mind, galvanizing me. *Why?*

Gareth knelt in front of me. Had I ever noticed before how cherubic he looked? I hadn't—my senses had been stolen by the master of Markham Hall the first night I'd arrived. But Gareth was handsome. Blond hair and blue eyes and a face that was so smooth and beautiful, it looked like a statue in the British Museum. He looked like an angel.

An angel who had tied me to a chair.

"I am really sorry about this, Ivy," he said. His voice was rather apologetic. "This was never my original plan—but I had to improvise after Violet's death."

I managed to raise my head a few inches, and then it bobbed back down.

"Do you know where we are?" he asked.

I shook my head.

"We're in Mr. Markham's Hampton house. It's quite a ways from London proper. It's where he and Violet shared their wedding night, you know." Gareth tucked a strand of hair behind my ear. "I was here for that too. I had to go in the valet's room in the attic and wonder if every creak, if every thump, was them making love. I'd been fucking her for two months by that point."

"You loved her," I managed. Somehow, I knew to keep engaging him, to keep feeding his tangential thoughts, even though the other parts of my mind that were firing into alertness begged me to find a way to end this madness. But how? My legs were free. That was quite an advantage. But I wouldn't be able to turn a doorknob with my hands behind my back.

"I did love her," Gareth mused. "I did. She didn't love me. But she could have. After she had our child, perhaps."

"Mr. Markham would have raised it as his own," I said. My mouth was feeling closer to normal again, my words coming out in my usual voice. "She wouldn't have risked falling in love then."

"I wouldn't have let him have the child. There was a time when I thought I might, when the thought of him raising my son was satisfying—fitting even, but I loved her too much. I loved her too much to let her be his. Even if she didn't want to be mine."

I didn't understand. Maybe it was the lingering effects of the agent he'd used to put me to sleep or maybe it was that none of this made any goddamn sense. Something about Gareth and Violet and the baby, but why was *I* here? Why was *I* involved?

And why was there a creeping fear that I would be made to suffer for someone else's sins?

"Do you know how I first met Mr. Markham?" Gareth asked, standing up. "Do you know *when* I first met him?"

"When you applied to be his valet?" It was a reasonable assumption, but it seemed to annoy Gareth.

"No. I had a life before working for Mr. Markham, you know." He started pacing. "I was born at the same level as him. I was born to a wealthy man and raised in a fine house. And I was but a boy when he married my sister. My *half*-sister," he corrected. "The first time I really saw him was at their wedding, at the York Minster, but before that, I felt like I knew him. My parents adored him. Arabella wouldn't stop talking about him. It was like he was part of the family before he'd ever even married into it."

Arabella.

Arabella.

The name almost didn't make sense. It didn't compute. Why

was Gareth talking about Arabella and Mr. Markham, why was he talking about a childhood growing up with the Whitefields . . .

"You were the Whitefield bastard," I breathed, realization clicking into place. "You were Josiah's son."

"See, you call me a bastard, but he never made me feel illegitimate, and neither did his wife," Gareth said. "I was educated and introduced to the finer members of society and groomed to inherit the estate. He never had a son with his wife, and he'd always planned to write me into the will . . . "

"But he didn't." Part of me sensed it was dangerous to be so blunt with him—he was clearly unstable right now—but the other part of me was desperate to piece together the reasons I was tied to a chair in an empty suburban mansion. I recalled all of Aunt Esther's tale. "He died before he could."

"Because Arabella died. Because Markham killed her."

"She was sick—"

"She was *alive* until she married him. She didn't worsen until after their wedding, until he dragged her all over Europe, and then she died, and left my father unable to cope."

"And then *he* died," I said softly.

"He died and his wife died, and the estate was sold off to the nearest heir, because I wasn't legally able to inherit. And then I was practically sold off as well. No one wanted me, no one would claim me. My birth mother was dead. Some distant relation of hers, a *farmer*, took me in and I was forced to finish my childhood among ignorance and poverty."

He stopped in front of me. "So do you see now? Do you see all he's taken from me? Not just Violet, but my sister, my parents, my home. All of it obliterated in the face of Julian Markham."

"So why would you want to work for him? If you hated him so much?"

"*Hate* is not the right word, Miss Leavold. Not at all. I never had a plan, I never had an elaborate revenge plot that I'd dreamed up like in the novels, but every major event in my life was tied to him, as if he were a port my fate had to return to over and over. I'd found work as a footman in my youth, and when I'd heard that Julian Markham was looking for a valet . . . it seemed like destiny. I didn't know why or what for, but I knew I had to. He didn't recognize me, of course. I doubt he ever paid much mind to his little bastard brother-in-law, and in case he had, I'd changed my name."

"So what . . . you were biding your time?"

"It's not like that," he said, almost impatiently, as if I were being deliberately obtuse. "I wasn't biding at all. I was working. I just felt like it was right somehow, that I should be close to him. I even thought that one day I would tell him my real name and he'd help me reclaim my place in the world. I'd never planned on doing anything injurious until . . . "

Until you fell in love with the same woman. I could see it now, the valet—overeducated and overbred, one small tragedy away from being at the same level in society as Violet and Julian—and then of course, Mr. Markham himself, wealthy and magnetic. Both handsome. Both attractive. Knowing Violet as I did, I wasn't surprised that she'd been unable to choose. Why not dally with the valet—who after all was born and raised a gentleman—while waiting to be made wife to one of the wealthiest men in the north?

And in true Violet fashion, she hadn't really loved either of them. It had been another game for her.

A game that had killed her in the end.

"I loved her. And I wanted her to bear my child." Gareth was truly agitated now, the pain of Violet's death clearly much more recent and raw than the death of his sister and parents. "And I knew, finally, what I had to do. It all became clear that night he caught us together. He had killed Arabella, and by extension, my parents. He was going to keep Violet and my child away from me . . . and then what he did to Violet after he found us, the things I heard coming from that room." He shuddered. "He deserved to die. He deserved it at least three times over, if not four."

"What did you do?" I whispered.

He met my eyes. "I knew I had to kill him, but I didn't have the stomach to do it directly. I went out to the stables and cut the cinch of Raven's saddle."

I stared back at him, understanding but not fully absorbing what he was saying. I had chosen to trust Mr. Markham. I had believed that he hadn't cut that saddle, that he wasn't ultimately responsible for Violet's death, but after that, I had let the matter lie, shoving the hand that had held the knife to the back of my mind. An unsolved mystery.

But here it was: solved, confessed, laid bare.

Gareth had done it.

"You killed Violet."

"No!" He was beginning to shout now, all pretense at calm abandoned. "*He* did! He killed her with what he did to her in that room. If he hadn't tormented her, she would have stayed inside where she belonged and *he* would have been the one dead in a field. *Fuck!*" He kicked viciously at a nearby end table, and it fell over with a crash.

I jumped in the chair, adrenaline singing through me, every nerve and muscle alive, every synapse firing. We were nearing the end of the talking time, I saw, moving closer to the reason he had brought me here. I wanted to fight and resist, to somehow bolt for the door, but I knew better. I needed to stall as long as possible, even as I realized there wasn't much point in it. Mr. Markham was detained by the police, and my aunt would have no reason to worry about me in the care of Mr. Markham's servant. The thought depressed me, scared me. No one knew where I was. No one knew that I was about to die.

But I had to try.

"I know you didn't mean to kill her," I soothed, hoping he couldn't hear the shaking in my voice. "No one blames you. It was an honest mistake."

"It was," he mumbled to himself. "But don't you see?" His voice grew plaintive, loud, discordant. "He's taken *everything* now—including the child I never got to meet. I am going to take something of his."

He stepped so close that his feet touched my feet, and my instinct was to hiss at him, like a cat, but I resisted. Instead I looked up at him. "This isn't necessary, Gareth," I said. "Please. I'm sure if you just explain it to Mr. Markham—"

"Explain what? That he deserves to suffer for what he's done to me? And what do you think he'll say in response? 'Yes, you're right, please take my fiancée'?"

That hadn't been what I'd meant, but I didn't know exactly what I *had* meant, only that I was trying to appeal to whatever sense of normalcy still lived in this man. This man who had seemed so sane, so damn sunny and friendly before. "There's got to be a way around this," I said. "What will killing me solve?"

Gareth shook his head. "Nothing. Absolutely nothing." He went over to the fireplace and started building a fire. "There's nothing that can fix what's happened to me. It's too late for that. But I can make sure that Julian Markham suffers like I suffered. And that will be a small comfort in itself, I think. All I really want is one glimpse of his face when he learns the truth. When he knows that you're dead."

"He'll kill you."

Gareth shrugged, still attending to his work. "He can try. I'm very good at hiding, Miss Leavold. I hid in plain sight for three years."

Whatever he was planning with this fire, I didn't like it. I tried to move the chair, gratified when I found I could force it across the low carpet with a minimum of noise. If I could make it to the door . . .

What then I didn't know. But damned if I'd sit here waiting to find out what happened if I didn't.

"I tried to save you, remember, the night he took you for his own? I tried to save you from being loved by him. I didn't want to hurt you. I *like* you. But I have no choice. You are the sacrifice with the most value. I delayed as long as I could, but then I realized that someone else in the house knew. I didn't have long before Julian learned who and what I was . . . "

The fire was catching now, licking at the sticks and logs in the fireplace, dangerously close to the pile of wood halfway in the fireplace and halfway on the hearth. I kept trying to move the chair as quietly as I could, having made it almost three feet since he'd turned away.

Three things happened at once then. The first was that Gareth stood up and turned around. The second was that I decided to run for it, no matter how hopeless it was. I stood in the chair and tried to run for the door as he chased me.

The third thing was that Mrs. Brightmore appeared in the doorway.

I blinked at her a minute, as I'm sure Gareth did too, her presence so incredibly incongruous with the setting and the circumstances that it was almost impossible to reconcile the two.

Oh, and she was holding a gun. A shot cracked through the air and plaster rained down, showering the room in granules of white dust.

Gareth froze behind me.

"Brightmore," he said, his breathing labored from his sprint across the room.

She walked farther into the room. "Sit down," she told me. I reluctantly obeyed. I wanted to keep running, I wanted to beg for help. I wanted to take her gun and shoot Gareth, but I sensed the wisest course was to make myself as quiet and as easy to forget as possible, so I sat, keeping my feet firmly on the floor as I did in case I got a chance to run again.

"Don't you want to know how I found out?" she asked Gareth. "That it was you?"

"I don't care," he said honestly. "It makes no difference now."

"I always recognized you," she said, continuing on anyway. "I knew you the moment you came to work at Markham Hall. But I didn't say anything. If you didn't want the master to know that you were Josiah Whitefield's bastard, that was nothing to do with me. But still—I watched you. You were a sneaky thing as a child, all dimples and bows for the lords and ladies, but devilish and cruel when they were out of sight. I knew what happened to those cats that ended up drowned on the Whitefield estate. To those outbuildings that mysteriously caught fire."

Gareth sounded impatient again. "I. Don't. Care. What. You. Know."

Brightmore didn't stop. "See, I thought the mistress was unhappy simply because of her marriage to Mr. Markham. But then I realized it was you. You were the one who made her unhappy. Who made her desperate for help."

Gareth shook his head. "She didn't give me a choice, Brightmore."

"She wanted to stop interacting with you. Wisely. But of course, you wouldn't let her stop, would you?"

"What did you do?" I asked, unable to help myself.

He looked down at me. "I did what I had to."

"He threatened to kill her. And the rest of her family—which is you," she pointed out, looking at me, "and she cared enough about you, for whatever reason, to comply."

Gareth took a step toward her. "How did you know that?"

"The same way I finally figured out that it was you who tampered with the saddle. Who's always awake in the middle of the night? Who is running inside and outside, up and down stairs, from three in the morning until nine at night?"

And then Gareth visibly paled.

"The kitchen boy," Brightmore said with cold satisfaction. "The police talked with Wispel, but they never spoke with him. And I began to wonder, what did you do after the master caught you that night? Where did you go? The kitchen boy had seen it all, running firewood inside the house. He saw you go into the sables. And he heard you threatening the lady all those nights. As soon as I spoke with him, I made plans to come to London. Mr. Markham needed to know."

Gareth was only a couple of steps away from her by now. "Why do you even care?" he said. "This doesn't concern you."

"Everything to do with my master concerns me." And in her eyes was the burning fervor of a religious convert. She raised the gun. "And while I don't care particularly what you do with the whore—"

It took a second to realize she meant me, but her words drowned out my noises of protest.

"—I do care that you tried to have the master arrested. And that you might try to kill him."

"It is a pity then," Gareth said, "that you won't be there to stop it." And he grabbed for the gun.

The moment I realized what he was about to do, I tried to stop it, flinging myself toward him. Another bullet fired, sending a wave of fear through me, and both the housekeeper and the valet fell to the floor in a tangle of limbs and skirts. There was shouting and grunting and the roll of heavy bodies on the floor.

I was on the floor now too, on my side, my breath forced from my body, all my weight on my arm, facing away from the struggle behind me. All I could see was smoke. The gray veil of smoke as the fire leapt from fireplace to hearth to rug. The house was catching fire.

The noises behind me died down, as if the struggle had stopped. I felt my chair move as Gareth stepped around me, gun in hand and blood running from his nose. He wiped at it with his shirtsleeve as he aimed the gun at me. "I was going to let the fire do its work," he said. "But now I think I shouldn't leave it to chance, don't you? We've had enough unexpected variables this afternoon—"

I kicked out viciously with my leg, making contact with his knee. He cried out and dropped and I kicked again, determined not to die passively. If I couldn't run, I would fight.

I kicked again and again, landing two or three good ones

before he managed to force himself to move through the pain, and then I heard an unearthly scream from behind me, like a banshee or a ghost caught by the sunlight away from its grave. A scream and then a roar as Brightmore came off the ground and charged at Gareth like a woman deranged.

He'd still been reacting to my kicks and so he didn't have time to duck or to dodge, and they both went flying backwards as their bodies collided, right into the trail of the fire.

Instantly, they both lit up, human pyres in a dark room, like ancient sacrifices in a wicker cage. The light was almost too bright to look at, searing and intense, and I could smell the distinct smell of burning hair and clothes and something sweet and meatlike that had to be flesh.

Gareth was screaming and Brightmore was still fighting him, even aflame, hell-bent on destroying the man who would destroy the only person she cared about. They were one indistinct pillar of fire now, and with a final scream that would haunt me until my dying day, the two of them careened toward the wide front window, crashing through the glass and to the sidewalk below.

Heart pounding, the sudden silence almost worse than witnessing the immolation itself, I squeezed my eyes closed and gave myself five seconds. Five seconds to be horrified, to want to run, to want to claw the very images out of my mind. Five seconds to be both grateful and confused and grateful again that this woman who hated me had sacrificed herself to save me—all for a love that would never have been returned.

Five seconds.

One.

Two.

Three.

Four.

Five.

I opened my eyes. The fire still burned, though now the smoke poured through the open window. But that wouldn't stop it from creeping toward me, no, I still had to get out. With a deep breath and a grunt, I started rocking the chair, straining to roll onto my front, so that I'd be on my knees. After several attempts, I managed it, my head knocking against the floor as I did and I finally managed the awkward half-standing position and moved out of the room.

Brightmore had left the door open and I emerged into the outdoors, where the sun had broken behind the clouds. The world was a brilliant blue, mild and breezy, October at its finest. All around me were leaves rustling, fine houses in the distance, and the still-smoldering corpses of the man who'd killed my cousin and the woman who'd stopped him from killing me.

EPILOGUE

JULIAN

*W*hat all I felt when I finally made it to my Hampton house and I saw the smoke and the swarms of police carriages, I don't recall. I remember panic, and more panic, and then rage at my delay in figuring out where Gareth had taken her. (Where else, once I'd thought about it. Where else would he have a key, where else to send a message to me?)

And what I felt when I leapt out of the Baron's carriage and saw my wildcat—her face covered in soot and tears, and two bodies covered with sheets beside her—but alive, yes, so, so alive.

Well, I still felt it. Every minute, every hour, a tidal wave of relief and thankfulness to whatever god still deigned to watch over me.

We'd waited two weeks to marry. Ivy was shaken after her kidnapping, and even though we didn't speak the thought out loud, it seemed strange to marry in the shadow of Brightmore's death.

Brightmore.

Even now, as I sat on the plush hotel bed in Paris, listening to the music of the city, I felt the weight of Brightmore's gift to us. Her death, her painful and absolutely unnecessary death. If only I had bothered to listen to her, to find her again! It was a self-flagellation that I couldn't stop. If only I'd been less careless, less selfish, Ivy would have never been in danger and Brightmore would be alive.

She had killed herself to save my wildcat. Because she cared for me.

And there was no way to repay her.

We'd decided to elope, out of England, somewhere far away from the painful memories that hung over us. But even though I'd told nobody where we were going, when we stepped into the small Breton chapel, I was still greeted by Silas's grinning face, by the Baron's serious but approving eyes. In the end, all of our friends—and Ivy's aunt—had joined us, even Molly, who actually seemed happy for us. And then we'd taken the train to Paris, to spend our wedding night there. Despite the tragedy of this month, I was starving for Ivy's body. Through all the arrangements and the sorrow, there'd been no chance for us to reconnect physically, and I had to admit, there was something prosaic about waiting until our wedding night.

But I'd done enough waiting.

Ivy stepped out from behind the screen, her wedding dress abandoned. She was completely naked, her breasts full and round, tipped with hard pink buds, her slender waist flaring into perfect hips and a taut ass. My cock, already half hard with anticipation, surged at the sight. God, I wanted her. I wanted to be inside her. I wanted to be biting her, sucking her, pounding into her . . .

I stood, but as I approached, I slowed down.

It had been a couple weeks since I'd seen her naked, but even at the Baron's, there'd been only candlelight and my mind had been . . . occupied with other things. But now, alone, in the light of the late afternoon, I could see something was different about her body.

"Turn around," I ordered.

She flushed with pleasure and complied, spinning in a slow circle. I walked up to her as she stopped and took her breasts in my hands, examining how ripe and heavy they were. Her breasts had always been perfect to me, but they were normally a little more than a handful. Tonight, they seemed much bigger.

I ran my hand down her stomach, normally so flat and smooth, and felt where it swelled ever so slightly, just above her pelvis.

"When was the last time you cycled, Ivy?"

She looked up at me, confused, her flush now one of embarrassment. Such things were hardly ever spoken of, even between man and wife, but I didn't care.

"I'm your husband," I said, letting a little sternness creep into my voice. "And we share a life. I will know everything about the body that houses this shared life, no matter how shameful you think it is. Now answer my question."

"It comes and goes . . . it's never been regular, ever since I started," she said, her cheeks burning now.

"Of course not, because you are terrible at taking care of yourself," I murmured, circling her body again. She hardly ever ate, she spent hours exerting herself, all things that women who wanted to conceive were counseled against.

Yes, from this angle I could easily see the small, firm curve of her lower abdomen.

"I suppose . . . this summer, maybe? I remember cycling before we had the visitors."

I was behind her now, and I slid my arms around her, letting my hands meet over that curve, my heart beginning to stutter with excitement. An excitement I never thought I would be able to have for my own. "I think we should send for a physician tomorrow."

"No," Ivy said disbelievingly, finally realizing which way my thoughts tended. "No, it can't be. I would have known, wouldn't I?"

I shrugged, moving around her again. I was only familiar with the barest parts of pregnancy, mostly from Silas's sister-in-law, who was constantly pregnant.

"Although . . . " she hesitated. "I have been feeling tired. And sick. Since I arrived in London, but I thought it was simply heart-sickness. Oh, God, Julian, a child . . . "

I stopped in front of her and then dropped to my knees. My face was level with her belly button, and I touched my forehead against her belly, breathing in and out as something so foreign I couldn't name it soared inside me, expanded until I thought my chest would crack open with it.

Happiness. It was happiness.

Unadulterated, untainted. Pure, blissful happiness.

I pressed my lips against her stomach, and she laced her hands through my hair, holding me there, and I suddenly felt like a penitent knight kneeling before a saint. My saint—my salvation—my perfect wildcat who now carried the most precious and tiny thing imaginable. In just a short month or two, I would be able to feel the child. I would be able to feel the kicks and the flutters.

"Julian," Ivy said, and I realized I was crying. No, weeping, my shoulders shaking, my breath hitching, completely undone by the most basic and elemental fact of life.

I kissed her belly, trailing my kisses down, suddenly desperate to show her exactly what it meant to me to have my child growing inside her. She had to know—had to *feel*—how happy and raw and grateful beyond words it made me . . .

I reached her bare cunt, pausing for a moment to breathe over the sensitive flesh. Tears still fell from my face, and when I looked up at her, she was crying too, but crying and smiling, and then I lowered my head and pressed my lips to her soft skin.

She shivered and I increased the pressure, parting my lips to flick my tongue across her clit, exposed and swollen. She sighed, and I nudged her legs apart, suddenly greedy for more. I smelled soap and a delicate smell that was all her own, and then I buried my face between her legs, sucking and kissing and laving her until I could feel her legs shaking around me.

I didn't relent, didn't let up, and kept going until she let out a soft cry and came on my mouth, the tender flesh quivering deliciously against my lips. I waited until the tremors subsided, then I stood and scooped her into my arms and carried her to bed.

I loved her like this, post orgasm, where she was so loose and sated that she could barely move. I loved that I made her that way. And I loved that the moment I started stoking her fire again, her hunger would return, more avid than before, and that's what happened now as I lowered my body over hers. She tugged and tore at my clothes, and I undressed as quickly as I could, eager to feel my body against hers.

I took her mouth, stroking into it with my tongue, and then I rubbed my bare cock against her sex, shuddering the first time it made contact. I flexed my hips, sliding the length up and down her folds, not allowing myself to plunge in—yet. No, I wanted her desperate before I did. I wanted her to come so hard that everyone in the hotel could hear it.

I lowered my head and sucked a nipple into my mouth, sucking until she gasped and squirmed and then I moved my attentions to the other one. I didn't stop until it was a stiff peak that brushed against my chest as I moved over her, and then finally, I notched the head of my cock at her entrance.

She lifted her hips to me, and I impatiently pushed them back down. She caught my hand with hers, her fingernails digging into the flesh of my wrist, and the bite of pain was what undid the last of my control, and I shoved into her as hard as I could, almost passing out from the feeling of her wet heat around my cock after so long.

I pulled out to the tip and then pushed in again, not fast but hard, just the way she liked it.

"Anything you want," I panted, so caught up with lust and

love and the fucking amazing sensation on my cock. "Anything you want and I'll give it to you. Let me do it to you."

She looked up at me, eyes full and deep. "Punish me," she whispered.

Fuck.

I pulled out and knelt between her legs. She looked perfect like this: legs spread, cunt wet, hair tangled. How would I manage to get anything done with her as my wife? I could barely bring myself to leave her now, to go get what I needed to continue fucking her.

"Don't move," I said hoarsely. She didn't, but her bright eyes followed me as I moved off the bed and toward the changing screen. I picked the dress off the floor, a very simple white affair that she'd chosen herself. I tossed it aside until I found her corset, with its long lacings, which I tore from their grommets. At the last minute, I picked the dress up again and divested it of the decorative ribbons that laced up the back.

When I returned to the bed, Ivy hadn't moved, but she trembled when she saw what I had in my hands. I made her sit up and then I tied her wrists to the bed, and then her ankles, leaving a little slack so that I could then wrap a length of ribbon around each of her thighs and then tie those ribbons to the bed frame. She was now completely tied up, immobilized, tied so that her legs were splayed open and her perfect cunt defenseless.

My cock was so hard it hurt, but I was determined to give her exactly what she asked for, so instead of plunging back inside her pussy, I moved up and knelt in front of her, angling my hips down so I could fuck her mouth. She opened her lips willingly for me, and I slid in. I waited until I knew she had consciously relaxed herself, and then I started going rougher, harder, driving in and out until her eyes started to water. I fucked her mouth until I heard noises, choking noises, and then I pulled out.

"Had enough?" I rasped.

She shook her head. "More," she said.

God, this woman. "I'm going to fuck your pussy now," I said. "And you're going to have no choice but to take it."

"As if I would want to do anything else."

I wasted no time once I got in position. I let go of all thought, all reason, and all inhibition, and I sank my cock into her as deeply as I could. I stayed there and then ground my pelvis against hers, putting an almost cruel pressure on her clit, rubbing and rubbing and watching her as she tried to squirm away and towards it in turns, watching her brow knit as she reached that place where she couldn't tell the difference between pleasure and pain any longer. Then I let go of everything all together and just fucked. As hard and as fast as I could. Hard enough to make her grunt and squeal and fast enough to strain the ties against her limbs.

I drank in the feeling of her soft thighs welcoming me, the sight of her tits bouncing frantically, the sound of her animal noises resolving into wild cries as she came around my cock.

My own release was coming, an explosion coiling tighter and tighter at the base of my spine. I was going to fill her with seed, I was going to fill her full of it, this cunt that had only ever known my cock, this cunt that I'd been the one to take first. I drove into her so relentlessly that tears sprang anew in her eyes and she was pleading for me to stop or slow down but she didn't say our safe word and so I kept going, reaching down to rub her clit into another climax. I was greedy. I wanted more from her. I wanted it all, everything, every atom of this woman's flesh, and she came again, crying openly now, and I was right on the edge.

"Come inside me," she begged hoarsely. "I need you to. I want to feel it."

"It's all yours, kitten," I said and then I inhaled sharply as it took me, an orgasm from hell, my cock convulsing so hard that I saw stars and my body was frozen in place, my muscles locked, and I realized I was growling through it all like an animal.

My hands still dug into her hips, and I forced them to relax. If I stayed in her much longer, I would get hard again, and since

I knew she would want me to fuck her again and again, I had to be the one to make sure her body got a break. She needed it, whether she thought she did or not.

"I want you to do that to me every day," she said, her voice small in that particular way that told me she was moments from sleep. "You have to promise."

"Oh, I promise." I pulled out of her and bent down to kiss her cunt.

"Good," she sighed happily.

"You are such a good pet," I praised her, untying her restraints next, making sure to kiss each and every red line the ribbons had left. But by the time I made it back to her face, her eyes were closed and her breathing had started to deepen. I smiled and brushed the tousled hair away from her face.

After I'd cleaned up, I crawled back in bed with her, even though I wasn't the least bit tired. I curled my body around hers, breathing in the sweet, clean scent of her hair, curling my hands protectively around her stomach.

I had wanted all of her just a moment ago, to consume her and to have her consume me in turn, and when we were fucking, sometimes it felt as if it would never be enough, as if I could never fuck hard enough to get as close as I needed.

But as I held her, feeling the swelling of promise in her abdomen, I realized that I did have her. Because I'd allowed her to have all of me. And we would continue on like this every day, each delight better than the last, each high higher than the one that came before it. I had my wildcat and she had me.

Forever.

THE RECLAIMING OF IVY LEAVOLD

CHAPTER 1

JULIAN

"Julian?"

"Wildcat."

"I think George is asleep."

I raised myself up on my arms to peer down at the baby nestled between us. We had taken our son out for a picnic today, and after Ivy and I had eaten and Ivy had nursed George, we'd all laid down on the blanket to stare up at the sky—George waving his tiny, dimpled hands the entire time.

But Ivy was right. With a belly full of milk and his mother and father on either side, he'd drifted off to sleep, his hands up by his round little head, his small curved lips parted. I could hear the barely audible snores issuing forth, and I adjusted the light blanket around his chest. Ivy said I was abnormally preoccupied with keeping him warm, but despite his chubbiness, he still seemed so small and fragile to me, even at four months old, and the thought of him being uncomfortable or unhappy for even an instant made me viscerally upset. So I made sure his every need was accounted for—that he only had the softest clothes, that he was never more than a few steps away from his mother, that Ivy had everything she needed while she rocked and nursed him in our room.

Ivy was curled around him now, looking up at me with the kind of wild look that made me wonder if she was all human, and I half imagined that if a stranger should stumble upon our makeshift den right now, then she would snap and snarl at him like a wolf.

It made me want to pin her to the ground and fuck her while she snarled at *me*.

In fact, my biggest struggle right now was that everything about Ivy—already perfect for me in every way—had somehow managed to become even more perfect since George was born. Her body, always beautiful, was now ripe and lush in a way that made me hard constantly, in a way I couldn't articulate to her whenever I tried. It had something to do with her fuller, heavier breasts, overflowing in my palms when I cupped them. And something to do with her hips that now flared enticingly out from her waist. And also the impossibly soft skin of her stomach, etched with slowly silvering marks that evoked the primal nature in me, because *I* had caused those marks, and it made me want to plant my seed in her again and again and again.

But more than her new body, it was *her*, her fierce maternal protectiveness, the frankly spiritual way she and George were bound together—it was impossible to explain without being either completely carnal or completely maudlin and so I gave up trying. Instead, I had tried to show her with my lips, with my hands, and—after the physician had given his consent—in a deeper fashion, although I'd be lying if I said that things had been the same after George's birth.

How could they be?

But how ironic that when I desired her the most, she seemed to desire me the least.

"Come here, Ivy," I murmured and she did, although not before kissing the tufts of George's raven hair and adjusting his blankets.

She crawled over to me and I pulled her down, so that she was flat on her back and I was propped up by her side, able to caress her neck and collarbone. But the moment I reached for the hem of her skirt, a tension settled over her that I'd gotten used to these last few months, a whole-body anxiety that had never troubled her before, even when she was a virgin. I'd tried to coax her past it, tried indulging this new fragility, tried talking around it, but it hadn't abated in the twelve weeks since we'd resumed having sex and I was starting to worry that maybe it never would, that maybe that part of my wildcat had died the moment George had been born.

"Be honest," I said, looking into her dark eyes. "Does it still hurt? I can use my mouth . . . "

She shook her head, closing her eyes. "It doesn't hurt. Go ahead."

Go ahead?

Like I was a customer at a brothel and she was just the forbearing servicer? What the *fuck*?

No. No, that was not going to stand. Not with me. Not today.

I pulled my hand out from under her skirt and pinned both of her wrists above her head, rolling on top of her to keep her still while I spoke, my hard cock growing harder at the feel of her underneath me. "Do you think that you're just a machine to me? That I only want to fuck you in order to satisfy myself?"

She opened her mouth but I cut her off, leaning down so that my lips brushed the shell of her ear. "I'd rather use my handkerchief than an unwilling wife. Do you understand?"

"Julian—"

I rolled off of her, our perfect afternoon punctured by my frustration. Mostly with myself.

George stirred, legs beginning to kick under his blanket. I sat and scooped him up in my arms as Ivy watched, cradled him one-handed as I gathered the remains of our picnic back into the basket.

"The sky looks like rain. I'll meet you inside," I said, not bothering to modulate the shortness in my voice. I regretted it the moment I saw Ivy look away, blinking quickly and clearly stung by my tone.

Fuck. Just—*fuck*.

A moment ago, we'd been in a dreamy summertime heaven, us and the perfect creature we'd made together, and now I was angry and she was hurt and the baby was awake, so I couldn't address any of it.

George yawned and then made one of those soft cooing noises that babies make, which undoes every wrong in the world. I melted. This was my wildcat, the mother of my child, and I would learn to be patient with whatever this was, and to do that, I first needed to apologize, although the idea of apologizing for telling the truth chafed at me. Not only because of my pride—well, perhaps a little bit because of my pride—but because we'd learned the hard way that honesty was the only way forward for us. So before George, I would have spanked her for being so distant with me. I would have fucked her until every confession, fear, and fantasy poured forth from her soul, and I would have punished her until I saw my bride flicker back to life.

But this was after George, and after George had new rules I didn't understand yet.

"Wildcat . . ."

She'd stood and was now folding the blanket, facing away from me. "It's fine." She turned, tucking the blanket into the basket. "You're right. It does look like rain. We should get moving."

* * *

136

THAT NIGHT, after Ivy and George had fallen asleep, I went downstairs to the library, where I poured myself a glass of scotch and sat down behind my desk.

A headache had remained after the picnic, dull and low, making me irritable all through dinner and beyond, and I'd done my best to stay quiet and out of the way, lest I wound Ivy's feelings again.

But it wasn't in my nature to be quiet and out of the way. It wasn't in my nature to let things fester and lie hidden. This current situation was untenable and it had to be rectified, but I, for once in my life, had no idea how to proceed. I stood and paced around the library.

This was where I had first kissed Ivy. I'd wanted to stop myself, I'd wanted to hold back, because she'd been placed in my care and it was my job to protect her from men like me. But God, she'd been so delicious that night, so full of righteous fury when she'd slapped me, her eyes blazing and her lips parted . . .

Well, it was no wonder I'd fallen for her, was it?

My dick stirred at the memory, and part of me debated simply using my hand to relieve this growing ache—it seemed wrong to go wake Ivy when she and George were asleep, just to coax her into doing something she'd be reluctant to do. I got as far as unbuttoning my trousers and closing my fist around my cock when I realized exactly how ridiculous I was being right now. Masturbating like a schoolboy when my lovely wife was upstairs, just as unhappy as I was, and rather than face our problem head-on, I'd rather skulk down to the library and come into my handkerchief.

How furtive.

How *pointless*.

Determination settled itself like a pile of coals in my belly, hot and urgent. Where was the man who'd claimed the wild and untamable Ivy Leavold? Who'd won her love and trust? Had he died at our son's birth too?

No.
No, he had not.

CHAPTER 2

IVY

*G*eorge was the perfect baby.

I knew very little about babies, but I was given to understand that they cried often, slept never, and that I would need a nurse to help me with mothering. But I refused to allow Julian to hire a nurse; the moment George had peered up at me with those huge, wise eyes, I knew there was no possible way I could let another woman care for him. He was *mine*, and like any mammal with her young, I guarded him jealously. Julian was allowed into our little world, of course, but even then, I sometimes felt like he was only a half presence, like a shade hovering at the edges of the only sphere that was real: George and me.

And I hated that. But at the same time, I didn't know how to invite Julian in. I would think about going to him during the occasional lazy spell in our afternoons, but then George would wake up from his nap. I would want to enjoy dinner with him, but then George would nurse relentlessly the entire evening. And at the end of a long day of changing diapers and swaddling clothes, of nursing and playing, I would sometimes just want to be *alone*, by myself and without a single soul having any claim on me or my time . . . even Julian.

So the first time we'd made love after George was born had been difficult for me. I was sore, yes, but that wasn't the problem. It was more like I couldn't bring myself to be present, like I had already bled all of myself out for George and I had nothing left to bleed for my husband and certainly nothing for myself. But I wasn't a fool—I knew that Julian needed sex the way most men needed food.

The way I'd used to need it, before the baby.

I had never wanted to be one of those meek, frigid women. But I didn't know how to stop it, and the more gentle and patient Julian became with my reluctance in bed, the more I pulled away, which made no sense, I knew, but it still happened. As if his patience and tenderness exacerbated everything I had come to dread about sex—mostly, that I had to service my husband's needs along with my baby's and I couldn't. I couldn't be everything for everyone, I couldn't give and give and give of myself endlessly, and not ever be replenished, but when he was so kind and so attentive, it made my selfish needs feel all the more selfish, because what woman wouldn't want a husband like my Julian?

* * *

WHEN I WOKE the next morning, George was stirring in my arms, rooting into my chest, and with a yawn, I sat up and nursed him through the vent in my nightgown, running the fingertips of my free hand over the soft crown of his head. He looked up at me, one chubby fist reaching for my face, and I caught his fingers with my lips, nibbling on them until he pulled off and made the squeaky, chuckling sounds that were his laughs.

I heard a deeper laugh from the corner of the room, and I

turned to see Julian observing us from an armchair, his head braced against his hand. "I love his laugh," Julian said. "Do you remember how at first, he'd only laugh in his sleep? And now he laughs all the time."

I nodded, looking back down to George, who'd started nursing again and who'd also decided that he was no longer sure about being awake. His eyelids had closed and after a few more pulls, I recognized the lazy half-sucks of a sleeping baby.

I raised my eyes back to Julian, to remark on George's predictable display of sloth, but when I caught his gaze, my throat went dry. I don't know how I knew it—how I could even tell the difference—but I did. The adoring father was gone. In his place was a man I hadn't seen in months.

"Put George in his cradle, Mrs. Markham."

His voice—raspy and authoritative—was also ice cold, the same voice he'd used whenever he punished me, something that hadn't happened since before George. And the *Mrs. Markham*— so distant. So demanding.

I shivered, fear lacing my blood, but I did as I was told quickly and without question, settling the snoozing baby in his cradle. After I finished, I turned and faced my husband, who made an impatient gesture indicating I should come stand before him.

Even in my nightgown, I felt completely naked as I approached his chair, even more naked as his eyes raked indifferently over me.

"Take it off," he said.

I quickly shrugged out of my nightclothes, eager to make that look go away, eager to see his eyes blaze with lust instead of this hooded displeasure. But once it was off and he examined me from head to toe, I was given no reaction, no appreciation, not even a flicker of interest.

"On your hands and knees, facing away from me," he commanded, and I obeyed, my cheeks flushing with hurt and shame and—as I assumed the desired position and as a bored foot nudged my knees farther apart—arousal.

He wasn't touching me, he wasn't talking to me, and since I couldn't see him, he possibly wasn't even looking at me, but all the same, heat flooded my body, the humiliation of this position quickening my breathing, setting my pulse to a thready race.

I waited, waited with an agonized sort of desire, waited for him to spank me or caress me or speak to me, but there was nothing, no movement, no rustling, no indication that he even cared about me arranged before him like this, my pussy exposed and growing slick with want. For the first time in I couldn't remember how long, I wasn't thinking about the baby, I wasn't feeling heavy and ripe and soft—too soft to be touched. I wasn't thinking of Julian's needs. I was only thinking of my own needs, my swollen clit and my tight nipples, and there was a high whine building at the back of my throat, a needy noise that I couldn't stop.

Why wouldn't he fuck me? For once, I wanted this—wanted *him*—and he was just sitting there, looking at me. Where had that gentle, patient lover gone, the one who had seemed so intent on pleasuring the mother of his child? I was ready for him, and he had gone away, and now I was miserable with the need to be fucked.

"Two things," Julian said, breaking the silence. "Two things will change, starting today. First, every morning I will dress you. Do you understand? Not your maid, not yourself. Me."

I shivered. The last time he had dressed me, he'd spent the day depriving me of sex . . . only to share me with his best friend later that night.

"The second thing. You will give me one hour of your time, every evening. No questions asked."

This, I balked at. "But George—"

He brought his hand down against my ass and I yelped.

"I said no questions." His hand stayed against the spot he'd just smacked, and I found myself pressing into his touch, wanting more. "But since I think you should know the arrangements I've made for this, I will tell you," he said. "I've hired a nurse, for that one hour only. She used to mind Silas's nieces and nephews, but she moved back to Stokeleigh to care for her mother, and Thomas and Charlotte Cecil-Coke gave me a glowing recommendation of her."

Some strange woman was going to take care of my baby? No. No, I didn't like that idea at all. What if he needed to nurse while she was with him? What if he needed to nap and she didn't know the way he liked to be rocked by the window?

No, that would not do, but the moment I opened my mouth to protest, Julian was down on the floor with me, his hand clamped over my mouth so I couldn't speak.

"Now, before you object, Mrs. Markham." He leaned forward to speak in my ear. "George is my son, my heir. Do you really think that I would entrust him to someone who wasn't completely vouched for and completely capable? Do you really think that my love for him is so much less than yours?"

I suddenly felt ashamed. Julian was right. He wouldn't hire a nurse that couldn't care for George as well as we could. And George was old enough that he could easily go without nursing for an hour.

He released his hand from my mouth. "For this one hour, wildcat, you will be completely mine. To do with what I want. Your mind and your heart and your body. They will be with me and nowhere else. Is that clear?"

I nodded, and another *crack* sounded through the air. I moaned.

"I want to hear your voice. Now answer me—are my directions clear?"

"Yes," I whispered.

"Good. Now stand up. It's time to get dressed."

"Dressed?" I whimpered, knowing what that meant. That meant no relief for the swollen ache between my legs.

"I won't ask again."

I stood unhappily, as he went and gathered my clothes. He dressed me then, and with a casualness that was almost cruel, he let his hands graze against my sensitive skin as he worked. His fingers brushed past my stiff nipples, lingered around my thighs, and after he laced my nursing corset tight, he grabbed me by the waist and pulled me into him, so that my back was pressed to his front, his erection grinding against my ass.

He wrapped his fingers in my hair and yanked my head to one side, and then he bent forward and scored the skin there with his teeth, biting and sucking and nibbling from my ear to my collarbone until I was slumped against him, knees weak and panting hard.

And just as quickly as it started, it stopped, his wicked mouth moving away from my neck. I whimpered again, but he paid me no mind, tugging a dress over my body and deftly wrapping my hair into an elaborate bun, which he quickly pinned up.

"I have some business to attend to in Scarborough today, so I won't be back until dinner," he told me, stepping away and eyeing my form, as if to admire his handiwork. "Bessie Knope, the nurse, will be here shortly before dinner, and I've already directed our housekeeper to acquaint her with the house and George's nursery when she arrives. All I require is that you be in the dining room at seven. Understood?"

"Yes."

He gave a short nod and grabbed his jacket from where it had been slung over the chair. He walked out of the room, pausing only to drop a tender, affectionate kiss on the sleeping George's forehead, and then I was alone.

* * *

BESSIE KNOPE ENDED up being precisely the person I would have myself hired to take care of George. She was a plump, patient woman in her fifties, and when she took a squirming George into her arms and started crooning to him in a soft, playful voice, the pair bonded so quickly that I almost felt jealous. But any jealousy I might have felt was immediately quashed by the insatiable, unbearable lust that had dogged me all day. More than anything, I wanted Julian to come home, drag me into the library, and fuck me until I was too sore to walk.

That's not what happened.

At seven, right after nursing George and handing him off to Bessie, I sat in the dining room, my heart pumping fast. I wanted Julian—I wanted Julian's body—but I was also nervous. Wary. A little frightened of him even. And that made me want him all the more.

But when he came in to the dining room, he came in with a packed basket of food and handed it to me, along with a pocket watch. I looked up at him, confused.

"Your hour . . . or rather, *my* hour . . . tonight will be spent alone by the stream in the woods."

I blinked, still not understanding, and he smiled.

"You have spent every waking and sleeping moment with George since the day he was born. But I remember a woman who longed for freedom, for the outdoors, for time to ramble and explore on her own. So tonight, you are your own dinner partner and your dining room is the forest you love so much. I'll see you in an hour."

"You don't want . . . ?"

He took me by the hands and helped me up, pulling me tight to him. "What I want," he said into my hair, his chest rumbling against my cheek, "is for you to do as I say before I spank your ass for disobedience. Now go."

Heat flared in my core at his words, but the stern expression on his face told me not to test him, at least not yet—although I'd be lying if I said a part of me didn't want to. Wanted to say no, just to see what he'd do. Wanted to defy him right up until the moment he held me down and pushed his cock inside me.

Then I heard a squawk from George—he and Bessie were in the parlor—and even though it was a happy squawk, it still brought everything else crashing down on me. The exhaustion, the exhilarating joy, the feeling like every nerve I had was scraped open and exposed. What was I thinking, gallivanting off for dinner by myself when I should be with my baby? Or if not with him, then attending to Julian's neglected needs?

My husband saw my hesitation, and his features grew stormy. "Go," he said, and his voice brooked no argument. I went.

When I came back an hour later, Julian was reading the paper in the library while Bessie rocked a sleeping George nearby. I'd spent the first part of my hour away fretting and feeling guilty, but then the summer evening had been so sticky and hot that instinct had taken over and I'd gone for a long swim, and as I entered the library, I felt cooler and fresher than I had in weeks.

Julian folded the paper down and looked over the top, smiling when he saw my wet hair, and then flipped the paper back up to continue reading. And later that night, after George was asleep, rather than let him stay curled next to me, I tucked him in his cradle and turned to Julian expectantly . . . only to find that he too was fast asleep.

Fuck. Fuck fuck fuck. Would he be angry if I woke him up? Would he be angry if I took care of this need myself?

But I didn't want that. It wouldn't be the same, not without him, not without his muscled form moving over me, driving into me. Not without his fingers twined in my hair and his low rasping voice in my ear.

So instead I settled myself against the pillow and stared at him, for the moment content simply to run my fingers along his naked chest, to trace the perfect, stern profile of his face with my eyes. This man, this grim, brilliant, attentive man. What was his plan, sending me off by myself? How had he known that I would enjoy it so much?

I fell asleep that way, staring at him, timing my own breaths to the slow measured rhythm of his and feeling more like myself than I had in a long while.

* * *

THE NEXT FEW days passed in a similar fashion. I would wake up, nurse George, and then be dressed by my husband. He'd abandoned the casual touches of the first day, and now was shamelessly torturing me—rubbing my clit before he pulled on my stockings, tweaking my nipples before lacing up my corset. But again, at night, rather than use our hour alone for dealing with the lust that he'd created, he'd sent me off alone. One night to read, another night to walk in the garden, another night to nap in front of the library fire.

And after four days of this, I was done. *Done.* Arousal clung to me like a haze, and I couldn't shake it off. I couldn't think, I couldn't reason, all I could do was watch Julian like a starving predator as we went about our days. Watch the narrow hips under his pants, the tight forearms when he rolled up his sleeves. The stubbled line of his jaw as he answered letters and bounced the baby on his knee while he read.

That evening, I sat in the dining room at seven, fully expecting to be sent off on my own again and dreading it. The hours by myself had been amazing—relaxing and clarifying and peaceful—and each time I'd returned to my family, I'd been so incredibly grateful for Julian orchestrating all this. But now that I had regained my equilibrium, begun to remember who Ivy was beyond being George's mother, I remembered who else Ivy was. She was Julian's wildcat, and without him, nothing felt right.

"Mrs. Markham," Julian said to me as he walked into the dining room. "You may stand. That chair will not be necessary."

Confused, I stood.

He turned to our new butler. "Please arrange for my dinner to be brought in, and only my dinner. Mrs. Markham shall eat hers later. And after the meal is served, I'd like this room cleared, and there are to be no interruptions for the next hour."

If the butler found anything odd with these directions, he didn't show it. Instead, he hurried to obey, the door swinging shut behind him.

My chest tightened with excitement, my stomach doing flips as Julian went to the clock on the dining room mantel and checked his pocket watch against it.

"Am I staying here tonight? With you?"

"Oh, yes, wildcat, you are staying. Do you remember our signal?"

Our signal. The word I would speak if the pain—physical or emotional—grew too much for me.

"Bluebell," I whispered.

The pocket watch shut with a click and he turned. He was already hard, his dick a thick ridge straining against his pants, but the rest of him seemed completely composed, completely in control.

"I hope you'll keep that word close at hand, my wife." His eyes glinted green in the candlelight. "Very close."

CHAPTER 3

JULIAN

*M*y meal was brought in, and after my plates were laid on the table, Wilson bowed and left the room exactly as I had asked. I locked the door behind him and turned to face my wildcat, whose cheeks were deliciously stained with color. Color that I'd put there with my days of teasing and torture.

I walked over to her and lifted her chin with my finger, examining that blush like an artist would examine his painting, pleased with the effect the flush had against her skin, my cock swelling at this small thing.

I wasn't blind—I'd seen the need building in her the past few days, like a geyser threatening to erupt—and it was entirely on purpose. Her words the other day by the stream, *go ahead*, had unlocked something in me, some determination, some need to master her that had laid dormant since George's birth.

Go ahead.

It was almost like a taunt, a dare like the kind she used to give me, and I had never been one to turn down a dare. And so that night when I'd stayed up late in the library, determined to find a way out of this, I'd listened to the darkest parts of myself. The parts that could sense what she needed from me, the parts that delighted in the idea of giving her those things.

And bit by bit, I had resurrected my wildcat, summoning her back to life like a magician summons a shade. Night after night, she came back to me and George with more of that feral perfection in her face, and night after night, I witnessed her frustrated desire growing and growing until she was practically frantic with it.

I had coaxed her back from whatever place she'd gone, and now it was time to remind her of why she would stay.

I let go of her chin.

"Mrs. Markham—" I loved calling her that, calling her by my name, and I especially loved it in moments like these, moments laced with discipline. "—there will be no need for your dress either. Please take it off."

Her breath caught, and she hurried to obey, fumbling with her buttons and ties as I sat and picked up my wineglass, adjusting my erection as I did so. I held the glass by the stem, pretending to watch the swirling liquid while really watching her. Her long neck, her strong arms. Her delicate shoulders appearing from the husk of her discarded dress. The compressed curves of her breasts and the narrow lines of her waist.

She was undeniably beautiful like this . . . but she was more beautiful naked. I wanted all of her newly ripe flesh available for me to squeeze and plump, I wanted to run my fingers over every inch of soft skin, I wanted to trace the marks on her stomach, knowing that I put them there when I planted my child in her belly.

"Continue undressing, Mrs. Markham. I'll wait."

I savored my wine—a good red, laid down by my grandfather

—and watched her progress, watched as she shucked her snowy white nursing corset and lace-trimmed petticoats until she was fully exposed to me, the flush on her cheeks mirrored by the one creeping up her chest.

Finally, she stood completely naked, too aroused to be shy, too far gone in her own lust to question me.

Which was exactly what I wanted.

"Bend over the table, Mrs. Markham. No, not there, here. In front of me. I want to see your cunt while I finish my wine."

Slowly she stepped in front of me and slowly she bent over, stretching her arms out in front of her so that her back was flat enough that I could have balanced my wine glass on it if I'd wanted to. The table was just high enough that she had to stand on the balls of her feet to bend at her hips, and I wanted to devour the lines of quivering muscle that ran from her calves to her ass and then press my face between her legs and devour the silky wet heat there. And then I would stand up, unfasten my trousers, and stab into her without any warning . . .

I ran a palm over my throbbing hardness, letting out a silent breath and willing myself back to complete self-control. I had denied myself these past days along with her, and I was full to bursting with the need to fuck this woman.

But the need to punish her was stronger, and so I would wait. I would feed the monster before I fed the husband.

I took my time finishing my wine, enjoying how every moment without my touch, without my voice, seemed to unravel her. I could see her fighting the urge to turn her head and look at me, biting her lip to keep from speaking, which was a very good wildcat, very good indeed.

I drained the wine and set the glass down as I stood up. I had planned on eating my dinner at a leisurely pace, on making her suffer more, but I couldn't sit still a minute longer with her like this: legs shaking, ass up, pussy so close and so, so inviting . . .

I unknotted my tie, grateful she couldn't see how painfully

hard I was, how my fingers shook as I yanked the fabric away from my neck. I managed to master myself enough to keep my hand steady as I ran it up her flank and over the curve of her ass, up to the delicate nape of her neck.

"Ivy Markham," I said, said it as if I were introducing her to an audience. "Ivy Markham. My *wife*."

Her control fractured and she turned her head to peer up at me, her dark eyes wide and pleading. If I hadn't already been hard, that look would have done me in.

She shrieked as my hand came down on her ass, hard enough that it stung my palm and I could see the livid lines of each finger on her skin. My cock twitched against my trousers, begging to be let free. I spanked her again, and again, and again, my breathing growing more ragged with exertion and arousal, my stomach clenching into a hot fist of angry desire.

I was angry. Yes, I could feel it, such a twin passion to lust, both so fiery, so energetic, both restless, agitating, primal feelings.

She could feel my anger too, I could tell, as her ass glowed red. Tears were sliding slow and silent from her eyes, dripping onto the tablecloth, and God, I wanted to lick those tears. I wanted to swallow her cries. I never considered myself a sadist —I preferred control, not pain—but in that moment, where the cost of four months of alienation and longing finally reared its ugly head, there was something so deeply, deeply moving about her offering physical pain to me, about her letting me exorcise this on her willing body. It scratched an itch somewhere so deep inside that I hadn't known it was there, and I felt drunk with the relief of it.

I paused my work and took a deep breath, closing my eyes for a minute. Not because I was afraid of hurting her—she knew what to say to get me to stop—and because even as undone and raw as I was at this moment, I still knew her limits and my own strength. No, I needed a moment because if I kept going, I was going to abandon all of my plans and fuck her right now. And while I knew it would be delicious and healing, I wanted more than healing. I wanted renewal. I wanted rebirth.

When I opened my eyes, they fell on the bottle of oil near the center of the table, kept for vegetables and bread, and I entertained the brief but intoxicating fantasy of drizzling that oil on her most intimate parts, of working it into her ass and then fucking her there in a fit of hot, slippery glory.

I forced myself back. *The monster before the husband*, I reminded myself. There would be time for both.

Instead, I bent myself over her body, pressing my rigid dick against her naked ass as I spoke low in her ear. "All this time that you've been lost to me, you've never spoken your signal."

My face was so close to hers that I felt rather than saw the confusion break through her mindless sensation. "What?" she asked, voice cracking.

I let my fingers trail over her hip and then back down to her ass. I slid my hand between my pelvis and hers, finding the tight, dry pucker I'd just fantasized about, and then dropping farther down to her slick, swollen cunt.

"Think about it, Mrs. Markham. All the times you shut yourself off from me, all the times in the past four months that you've laid back and thought of England instead of your husband—why did you not simply tell me *no*? Why not use your safe word, when you knew that I'd always honor it?"

"I . . . " her voice was shaky and indistinct, as if she were struggling to formulate thoughts. "I . . . wanted to be a good spouse. I wanted you to get what you needed."

There . . . I found her clit, now a ripe little bundle, practically begging to be rubbed, pinched, plucked. I grazed a fingertip past her, so lightly as to barely touch her at all, and she moaned loudly into the table.

"See, I don't think that's true," I told her. "I think that's what you told yourself. I think that's maybe even what you still believe. But deep down, there is another answer. The real answer. Do you know what it is?"

I shoved two fingers past the soft lips guarding her entrance, shoved them in deep. She moaned again, rolling her face against the table.

"I don't know," she managed, her feet scrabbling adorably at the carpet in her effort to open her legs wider, raise her hips higher to me.

"Yes, you do." Leaving my fingers in her, I straightened and used my other hand to smack her ass again. She gasped, and then I took my fingers from her pussy and rubbed around her other entrance, using her own wetness to ease a finger inside, then two. She was trying and failing to catch her breath, her fingers turning into claws, twisting into the tablecloth. Wine glasses and vases of flowers were knocked over, and the sound of that coupled with the feeling of her ass like a scorching furnace around my finger was enough to break my resolve. *Just a touch.* That wouldn't throw anything off, certainly, just a few strokes in and out to head off this desire and keep my head clear.

I reached down and unfastened my trousers, my dick tilting forward, but still pointing almost straight up. In a moment's work, I had the oil in hand and spread around the crinkled skin, my shaft also covered with a glossy sheen, ready to take her dark flesh.

I pressed the head of my cock against her and she cried out.

"Yes," she whimpered. "Yes, yes, yes."

"Careful with that word, Mrs. Markham," I said, halting my movement. "You don't know what you're saying yes to."

"I'm saying yes to *you*, Julian," she said, and it was so open, so vulnerable, the way she said my name, that all of my anger and all of my lust was now bound up with the tenderest feelings that a person can have for someone else. My precious wildcat, my sweet wife, who I had vowed to take care of and who I'd failed these last months.

No more.

I gritted my teeth and leaned forward, the sensation of her

tight, tight skin giving way enough to make my balls tighten, and I wasn't even inside yet.

"You didn't answer my question from before."

I talked as I pushed, going so slowly that it would almost be like I wasn't moving at all, except I could see the incremental progress as her body swallowed my dick, took it deep within herself. She cried out as the wide crest of my cock finally pushed past the initial resistance. I gave a little hiss, but I continued with my lecture.

"You know what I think? I think you didn't use our signal because you wanted me to come after you. You wanted me to take you like you needed to be taken—roughly, without question, completely subject to my discipline. You needed me to crack open the shell of motherhood and let the wildcat back out, and instead, I let you fester inside of it."

I finally slid home, buried to the balls, and her skin was so hot, so tight, and would I ever get enough of every part of her? Especially now that her body was so much fuller, so much riper, a body that begged to be kneaded and worshipped—and fuck, she was bucking into me, her body stroking me as I stayed still, and I was going to come right here and now if she didn't stop, I was going to shoot my load in her beautiful ass, and I had other plans for it . . . and for her.

I pressed the flat of my palm against her back. "Be still, Mrs. Markham. Or I will pull out right now."

She froze, but small sounds emitted from her throat that betrayed her abject distress.

"Now, where was I? Ah yes. You needed me, you were telling me precisely how you needed me by not using your signal, and I failed you. And for that, my wife, I am so, so sorry. It was my duty—my vow—to keep you and care for you, to break you and put the pieces back together every day for as long as we both lived . . . and instead, I coddled you. I treated you the very way you needed to be shown that you were not—I treated you as if you were fragile, as if you were powerless, as if you were weak. When all along, you needed me to show you how strong, how magnificent, how fucking beautifully powerful you are."

She was crying now, crying from my words instead of my hands, and I leaned over her again to slide my arms underneath her and raise her up to a standing position. I had to bend my knees to keep inside of her, but fuck, the change in angle and the weight of her breasts in my hands had me nearly weeping too, trembling with the urge to fuck her hard. Especially when I felt those breasts grow heavier, when I felt her shudder, and then felt the wet warmth of her leaking against my palms. I know many men shied away from this aspect of child-rearing, but I did not, because knowing that this sweet milky warmth was for the child that she had given me made me painfully, viciously aroused. The primeval male in me growled with pleasure, with the urge to sire more babies on her, with the blind need to spill my seed inside my mate.

Her letting down while I was in her ass made her cry harder. "Julian, I can't do this. I can't be both. I don't know where my heart is . . . "

I slid my hand up to press it against her chest. I wasn't pumping now; I was simply inside her, against her . . . *with* her. "Your heart is mine, Ivy. To do with what I will."

She sobbed at the sound of her name, which I had deployed intentionally—tenderly—because she needed to know that she was still Ivy to me—still my wildcat as well as my wife. "Your heart is mine. And George's. And your own. You are Mrs. Markham. And my wildcat. And Ivy Leavold. You can be all of these things at once."

"But how?" she pleaded. "How do I even start?"

"You start like this. *We* start like this." I kissed the back of her neck. "One hour at a time."

She didn't answer directly, but I could feel her answer in the way she pressed against me, the way her sobs turned to mournful hiccups. And that made what I was about to do feel so unfair, so cruel, given her fragile state, but it was for the best. And besides . . .

"Our hour is almost up, Mrs. Markham," I said and I pulled out of her, wincing at the loss, my entire pelvis throbbing with the need to fuck. Oh, how good it would feel to bend her back over and just pound my way into oblivion with no regard except for my need for release . . .

I turned her around, my own desperation somewhat alleviated once I saw hers scrawled across her face, alleviated with the tight stitch of love and adoration.

"You're not—we're—no, Julian, we can't stop like this." Her chin dimpled with more tears—frustrated ones—and there was a shine of fury in the back of her eyes that did nothing to diminish my raging erection. "You can't leave me like this, *again.* Tell me you aren't. Tell me that tonight you will finish this."

I buttoned myself back up. "I can't tell you that, Mrs. Markham. That would be a lie."

Pure rage spilled across her beautiful features, and a thrill zinged through me, straight to my balls. If I took her now—she'd scratch me and bite me and whisper dirty, angry things in my ear.

God, I would come so fucking hard.

It was that primeval man that stepped forward and licked—yes, licked, not kissed—the tears from her cheeks. It was him that ducked his head and ran his tongue around her erect nipple, tasting the sweet milk meant for his young. All of her—milk and tears, breasts and cunt, soul and mind—belonged to him.

Belonged to me.

"Get dressed," I said as I stood straight again, wiping my mouth with the back of my hand. "We only have about five minutes before Bessie will be expecting us, and I think she'd be rather shocked if you came before her like this."

"No," she refused. "Not until you fuck me, properly. I won't get dressed."

I raised an eyebrow. "I seem to remember you once daring

me to wrestle you into your clothes. Is this you making good on that dare?"

In the time that it took for comprehension to settle on her face, she was in my arms. She struggled, thrashing and strong, and it took a considerable amount of effort to keep her restrained while I scooped her corset from the ground and wrapped it around her waist.

"No," she was saying, "you can't."

"Do you have a word you'd like to say to me, wildcat?" I growled in her ear.

She stopped moving, just for a minute, which was long enough for me to hook the corset clasps in front. I used my own knee to buckle hers from behind, forcing her to the ground. She tried to wriggle free but I kept her on her stomach, planting a knee on her ass and a hand on her neck.

Goose bumps erupted all over her body, and she whimpered into the carpet, her hips moving under my knee as she ground her clit into the floor.

I slapped her ass. Hard. "I asked," I breathed, finding the laces to the corset with my free hand, "if you had something you wanted to say." I jerked the laces to tighten her corset, and she moaned, shaking her head.

Still holding her down with my knee, I tied the tightened laces in a bow. I looked down at myself; wrestling her into her corset, pinning her down with my knee, watching her reaction to being pinned down . . . I was harder than ever. I stood up as she rolled over, dazed, now half dressed.

"Bad wildcat," I said. "You've made me so hard. Come here and see what you've done."

She got to her knees, now kneeling right in front of me, and she pressed her cheek against my erection, rubbing her face against it like a cat.

"Please," she purred. "At least let me make you come."

Fuck, that was tempting. But no.

"The hour's up. Pull on your petticoats and dress and go

fetch George. I would, but . . . " I glanced down at my tented trousers. "I don't want Bessie to get the wrong idea."

A giggle—pure, wild, unladylike—escaped from Ivy's mouth, and I thought my heart would crack open with loving her so much. She was almost back.

CHAPTER 4

IVY

*J*ulian made good on his word. He didn't deprive me of his presence, but after George fell asleep and was placed in his cradle, Julian pulled me into bed and wrapped his strong arms around me, a gesture both loving and utilitarian—I couldn't move my arms to touch myself or him.

And even though his erection threatened to scorch an outline of itself against my ass, he didn't grind against me or make any move to seek relief for it. Instead, he buried his face into my neck and fell asleep, his warm, heavy breaths so intimately, wonderfully male, that I found myself smiling as I too drifted off.

But however intimate our sleeping snuggled together was, it was a paltry substitute for what I really needed, and I woke up the next morning to a hand grabbing my wrist. I opened my eyes to see Julian above me, George cooing on his hip.

My husband's face was stern, and I realized that I had been about to touch myself in my sleep. "Do I need to keep a watch on you at all hours, Mrs. Markham?" he muttered.

I sat up and he let me go. "Sorry," I murmured, reaching for the baby, who started babbling happily as soon as I took him and began the familiar motions of opening my gown.

Julian himself was only half dressed, wearing only his trousers, and I guessed that he hadn't been awake for very long. "What are our plans for today?" I asked, eagerly, hoping they involved the nurse coming early.

He shrugged on his shirt, the muscles of his stomach and chest and shoulders moving in a way that reignited everything in my core. "We will have our hour together at supper time."

"Not until supper?"

He grinned as he buttoned his shirt. "Are you so impatient?"

"*Yes*," I said empathically. "I am. What I am I supposed to do all day until then?"

"You'll find something, I'm sure." His face darkened. "Although, I will know if you've misbehaved, so bear that in mind, wildcat."

I shivered.

After the baby was finished nursing, I set him on the floor with his rattle and I approached Julian, who'd already laid out my clothes for the day, and I let him dress me. Today, his fingers were efficient and direct—no lingering, no grazing, no teasing. And somehow, that aroused me even further, the brush of his knuckles on my back as he pulled me into my corset, the brief touch of his palms on my shoulders as he spun me around. The rough tug of his fingers in my hair . . .

He leaned in to kiss me, and his lips barely touched mine before he pulled away.

I wanted to sob at the unfairness of it all.

* * *

THE DAY WAS MISERABLE. There was no way around it; out of all the miserable days I'd endured in my lifetime, this was in the top ten. George, at least, was as easy as ever, and I finally contented to spend the day splashing with him in the shallowest part of the stream, where he could sit in my lap and grab at the water with his dimpled fists and squawk at any birds foolish enough to land near us.

The hours dragged on and on, my thoughts only about Julian, about being bent over the dining room table with his cock in my ass; about his deep, graveled voice in my ear, daring me to say my safe word; about his knee on my back as he laced up my corset.

And then, thank God, it was time to get ready for supper. I took a quick bath and washed my hair, and changed into one of my nicest gowns—a deep scarlet silk that was almost black in places—and a ruby and diamond necklace Julian had given me on the day George was born.

I gave George an extra squeeze as I handed him off to Bessie, and then I practically sprinted to the dining room, where I found . . . the butler.

I stopped short, breathing fast, as Wilson bowed. "Mr. Markham has requested that you join him on the fourth floor."

Oh thank God. He hadn't forgotten or deliberately delayed this very, very necessary interaction. I gave a quick *thanks* to the butler and then hurried up the stairs of the central tower, up to the rarely used fourth floor, which was nothing more than a square stone room hung with tattered tapestries, drafty in the winter and broiling in the summer.

When I arrived, Julian was standing by the window—an ancient thing of wavy, thick glass—the pink and orange light of the sunset coloring him into a vivid chiaroscuro painting. "Mrs. Markham," he said, turning toward me. "I have something I want to show you."

He extended his hand and I took it, and we walked over to a tapestry, which he pulled aside to reveal a thick wooden door, a door so old that it looked like it belonged inside of a fairy-tale castle. He pushed it open, and then we were in a small, narrow stairwell that led straight up, and when we reached the top, he pushed open a trapdoor, and we emerged at the very top of Markham Hall, standing among the crenellations that could be so easily seen from the village and the forest.

"This is amazing," I breathed, moving over to the parapet to look out over our land.

"You're amazing," he said, coming behind me and wrapping his arms around my waist. "And you're mine."

Oh, those words. No matter how many times he said them, they still struck at the very heart of me. I turned to face him, the parapet digging into my lower back, a thrilling jolt of adrenaline racing through me as I realized it was principally Julian's arms keeping me from toppling over the edge.

He lowered his mouth to mine, and no truncated, businesslike kiss for him; he parted my lips and licked past my teeth, his tongue sliding against mine in a way that reminded me of how that tongue felt between my legs, and I sighed against him as my lower belly caught fire with want.

And then he stepped back and his hands were on my shoulders, firm and not to be denied, and then I was on my knees, the rough stone of the roof catching on the silk of my dress. I didn't care. Let it be torn to shreds, let it be destroyed, all that mattered was my Julian, what he wanted. He took off his jacket and unknotted his tie, and then took off his shirt, and the fading light only served to highlight the flat, lean muscles of his stomach, the delicious V-shaped muscles leading into his firm ass and narrow hips.

I watched his cock slowly appear as he unfastened his trousers—the taut, straining head, the veined shaft—and then his hands were bracketing my face, and my mouth was full of him—the clean, soap smell of his skin, the slightly salty taste of his arousal.

I moaned at the taste and feel of him, at the rough way he fucked my mouth, shoving in farther than I thought I could take him, pulling out so fast that I barely had time to breathe before he pushed in again.

I missed this, I realized. I'd missed this so much and so deeply that I hadn't been able to articulate it to myself, hadn't been able to feel it as anything other than an empty restlessness in my soul. Julian was right—I *had* wanted him to reclaim me, I *had* wanted him to beat past all the minor burdens that came with changing into a mother and that added up, day after day, until they formed a wall that was almost impenetrable and dazzling in its height. I had needed him to break past that wall, tear it down brick by brick, and instead, he'd tried coaxing me over it, pampering me over it, when the real problem was that I couldn't climb it on my own. And so we'd been on opposite sides of the wall, him growing more frustrated and desperate, me retreating into myself.

As he continued fucking my mouth, growling things to me —*it feels so good* and *deeper, I need deeper*—and my pussy grew wetter and needier, I thought about how unique this situation must be. Most women, I supposed, needed precisely the tender attentions that Julian had tried to give me after George's birth. But I wasn't most women. I'd needed *this*, I'd needed last night. I'd needed to feel his discipline raining down on my ass in a series of sharp, stinging blows.

I moaned again, remembering the spanking last night, and the vibrations from my throat made Julian moan too. He pulled out, his dick glistening. "Lie down," he said hoarsely, and I did, my throat catching at the hungry way he got to his knees and dove for my skirts, clawing and pulling until his mouth pressed against my pussy in a searing kiss.

"Oh God," I panted, falling back, my legs falling open in a rustle of silk and lace. "Julian, if you don't stop, I'm going to—oh —please—"

He growled against my pussy, and I squirmed, panting, moaning, the sensation after so many days of deprivation too overwhelming to process. I could feel it, a tightening in my core, a cramping in my inner thighs, a quivering, poised thing ready to career over the edge. And just as I felt it start to abandon itself to gravity and fall, he raised up, the monster, and wiped his mouth, and the climax hovered just out of reach.

I whimpered. He grinned.

There was no shirt, no tie, to grab on to, so I reached up and dug my nails into his arms, trying to pull him down to finish the job, and when he wouldn't, I scratched my nails down his bare stomach as hard as I could. He hissed, the grin was gone, and then, without warning, he was on top of me, crushing me, his hand pinning my wrists above my head while his other hand was under my skirts, holding himself, positioning himself, and then there was the perfect, heavenly, sublime truth of his rigid dick filling me, claiming what belonged to him.

The minute he slammed into me, my back arched off the floor and I cried out into the twilight sky, and then I bit his shoulder to stifle the rest of my cries, not wanting the whole village to hear us. My teeth sent Julian into a frenzy, and he pounded into me with a ruthless cruelty that dragged my orgasm back to the edge, all the stronger for the serrated lines of pain that came along with it.

"Oh, I've missed this cunt," he grunted, his hips flexing hard and fast between my legs. "I've missed making it come."

I could barely breathe—each breath was driven out by the relentless stabbing of his cock as soon as it was drawn—and every muscle in my body was twined so tightly that I thought I would slice clean through myself with my own orgasm, and then he moved up my body just a few inches, just enough that his pubic bone ground against my clit with each thrust, and that was it. I came. I came with four months of listlessness and isolation behind it, with four months of tame, tender sex, and the brutal weight of him against my clit and the furious fucking he was giving my pussy washed it all away, until I was lost to myself, lost to the world, lost to everything except his cock filling me and the clenching, cramping waves of pleasure that it gave me. My climax ripped up through my chest and down to my toes, over and over again, and still he kept fucking me, fucking me right into my second orgasm.

"I'm going to come so hard," he grunted. "God, I can feel it. I wanted to come on your face, but I have to come in this perfect pussy, I have to, because you feel so fucking good."

His words sent me over the edge again.

He groaned as my body seized and shuddered around him for the second time, and then he thrust in so hard that my toes curled, and stayed there, swearing violently as he shot his seed deep, deep inside, his cock throbbing hot and hard in my pussy as he emptied himself, giving me everything he had.

We came down slowly, a tangle of sweaty limbs and wrinkled silk, and his stubble brushed against my cheek as he hung his head, panting.

"Mrs. Markham," he said in wonder.

"Mr. Markham," I said back, also in wonder, because now that we were here, it was so hard to understand why we'd wasted so much time over *there*, in that murky, unhappy place.

He rose up on his arms to look at me and brushed a strand of hair off my forehead. "Mine," he murmured, and I nodded.

"Julian, I'm—"

"Don't," he interrupted. "We're here now, and that's what matters."

"But—"

He silenced me with a kiss, a long, loving kiss that made tears come to my eyes and at the sight of my tears, he started thickening inside me again.

"But what if it happens again?" I worried as he lifted his head and gave his cock an experimental thrust.

"Then we know where to find the answer," he said, pulling out to the tip and stroking back in, each inch an excruciating delight against my sensitive inner flesh. "Between us. Like this."

"Okay," I whispered.

"On your hands and knees, wildcat."

I rose up to obey and as I did, he checked his pocket watch.

"Do we need to go get the baby?" I asked, settling my weight on my hands and sighing happily as he slid in, my eyes fluttering closed as he began to rut into me in earnest.

"Not yet. There's enough time for me to have you again."

"Mmm." I liked the sound of that.

"And then after the baby falls asleep, I'll have you again tonight. And again before the morning."

"*Mmm.*" I *really* liked the sound of that.

"And again and again, until you give me another child."

"Good lord," I protested. "Can't we hold off thinking about that, at least for another year?"

He chuckled and his hand dropped down to find my clitoris, rubbing it in tight expert circles as he fucked me. "At least give me another orgasm then."

I rocked back into him, my husband, my master, my teacher. My Julian.

"On that point, Mr. Markham, I think we can agree."

* * *

Thank you so much for reading the Markham Hall series! I hope you've enjoyed Ivy and Julian's dark and twisty story!

If you like your historical with plenty of kink, lots of heat, and twisty characters, then you'll love *The Seduction of Molly O'Flaherty...*

Keep reading to learn more!

READY FOR MORE STEAMY HISTORICAL ROMANCE?

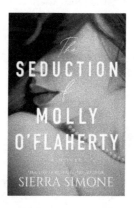

One playboy billionaire.
One heartbroken heiress.
One sham marriage.
What could go wrong?

—

That's what notorious playboy Silas Cecil-Coke thinks as he returns to England to persuade Molly O'Flaherty to marry him. Certainly, their brief fling last year ended in heartbreak (and a black eye), but matters are different now. Molly must marry to save her company, and Silas is determined that he'll be the man she chooses.

Between the bitter memories and the competing suitors, Silas discovers that wooing a bride is no easy task, unless, of course, he decides to stop playing fair...

Check out The Seduction of Molly O'Flaherty now!

"Sierra's books are like none I've ever read. **Compelling, full of imagination and even humor**, but in addition filled **with beautiful, brilliant, thoughtful-provocative** lines. You won't just read this or any of her stories, you want to both **savor and devour** them and enjoy them to the fullest."
--Avephoenix

"Fascinating! **Fantastic chemistry and heat!**"
--Bookworm

"**Sensual--Erotic--Emotional**..........This book is packed with **a whole lot of sexiness!!**"
-- DD, Amazon Reviewer

Treat yourself to more corsets and dirty deeds tonight!

ACKNOWLEDGMENTS

Thanks to Laurelin Paige, my universal constant. To Kayti McGee and Melanie Harlow, for all the Renaissance babies who can't even. To Geneva Lee, my first critique partner and best source of hard words.

To Tamara Mataya, editrix extraordinaire! Thank you for taking the time to make sure all the penises are grammatically correct. And thank you to Erica Russikoff of Erica Edits for giving me a final polish!

To all the ladies who shower me in blog love, thank you, thank you! To Jen, Angie, Tarah, Paula, and Candi, along with Angie and Jenna—you girls make it easy for me to come out of my introvert cave—especially when you make my books into such beautiful teasers!

And, on a more somber note, thank you to my mother, who died of breast cancer this winter. You never knew that I was writing smut before you died (which was probably a good thing) but I know you would have still have been proud in your own way. I probably wouldn't be the happy, raunchy, Scotch-drinking woman I am today if you hadn't given me free rein in the library as a girl and let me borrow all your old V.C Andrews paperbacks (in retrospect, probably when I was still a little too young for them.) This book was the first thing I wrote after you died, and it was the hardest thing I've ever written because I had to learn to believe in happy endings again.

I miss you. I hope there's Scotch where you are.

ABOUT THE AUTHOR

Sierra Simone is a USA Today bestselling former librarian who spent too much time reading romance novels at the information desk. She lives with her husband and family in Kansas City.

Sign up for her newsletter to be notified of releases, books going on sale, events, and other news!

www.thesierrasimone.com
thesierrasimone@gmail.com

Printed in the USA
CPSIA information can be obtained
at www.ICGtesting.com
LVHW091626090724
785039LV00022B/188